M

Edward L Hawke's

Great American
Screenplay

EDWARD L. HAWKE'S GREAT AMERICAN SCREENPLAY

WGA E Registration No. 142984
ISBN: 978-0-578-00473-0

PRINTED IN THE UNITED STATES OF AMERICA

M

Introduction

Josh Pinkerton

My dear old friend, Ed the Hawk, aka Edward L. Hawke, died this past year. He died the way he would have likely wanted. It was up on North Highland Avenue, in one of those chain-franchise hotel-motel places. He was sixty-six; the high-end call girl was about twenty-two. I met her a few days later and she was still in a state of weeping devastation. While we were at the mortuary, she described to me what a wonderful man 'Sweet-Eddie' was. I asked her why they met at a motel, when he had such a big, beautiful, empty mansion only a few miles away in Beverly Hills. She said that he just liked the ambiance of a motel. I sensed that the word 'ambiance' might be one she recently learned from Ed. She was right, though. Leaving his Beverly Hills home to meet a girl at a motel was his style. I tried to assure her that Ed lived a hard and unhealthy life and that it was amazing he had lived as long as he did.

Edward Hawke and I met over forty years ago in Vietnam. We were helicopter pilots in the 101st Airborne Division located at Camp Eagle. We were thrown together one weekend to fly a civilian consultant from Quang Tri to Da Nang. There was something odd about the entire thing. We were both aircraft commanders who would have ordinarily flown with lesser-qualified copilots. It didn't take long for us to figure out that we had been specifically picked for that flight.

That weekend we were sucked into the Military Intelligence Corps. There wasn't anything grand about the whole operation. At first, we were assigned to look into helicopter sling loads that were mysteriously and much too often being dropped in the wrong places. Before our tour in Vietnam was over, we began running short flights into Laos, across the DMZ into North Vietnam, and later into Cambodia. We were young and foolish and believed that this was as close to 'James Bond' as anyone could ever hope to be.

As soon as we got back to the States, we were both offered early discharge if we would sign up with Air America. At that time, Air America was an airline being operated by the United States Central Intelligence Agency. The salary was outstanding and we didn't have to pay any income tax. The one drawback was that we had to live in Thailand. I think Ed enjoyed it. I never liked the food or any of the smells.

My friend Edward Hawke loved being associated with the agency. I think if they had given him a job mopping floors he would have still loved it. The thing is, there was always something much more exciting being offered up. Looking back, now, I think that I would have dropped out and would have gone home. Ed kept wanting me to go with him on one more adventure. The events of our lives escalated from various small matters to larger and more dramatic actions. Even though our relationship with the organization after Air America was never formalized like typical employees, the agency began viewing Edward Hawke and Joshua Pinkerton as a matched set of contractors. Over all those years, we traveled the world and did a thousand things.

It was in the early 1970's that we were brought back to Los Angeles and left sitting around the pool doing nothing productive. While we were drinking, smoking, and living it up on our quasi-corporate-government checks, Ed decided to tryout for a part in a movie. I told him that I was certain that the agency would not be happy about one of their subs becoming a movie star. He wouldn't hear it. He got a very small speaking part. The

2

movie was called *Trafalgar*. It was a flop. Not only was the movie bad, but the late great Edward L. Hawke couldn't act his way out of a paper bag. I never told him that, but he knew it. It didn't matter; the movie business had a grasp on him that he couldn't shake. That was when he started writing his first screenplay.

While we were in South Africa, in 1975, he finished writing *Key West*. I frankly couldn't believe his success in selling it. He immediately started writing as though it was an obsession. Well, that's all history now. I felt sorry that Ed never got all the accolades that should have come with his success. He moved into the role of producer and later as director. In 1982, we were certain that he would be nominated for an *Academy Award*. Unfortunately, it was just as the nominations were being made that he was arrested.

Ed was driving from Miami Beach to the airport in a Hertz rent-a-car when he realized something was in the backseat. He said that he was still on the A1A when he glanced back and saw Pancho Baker's head sitting in the backseat. He swerved through the median, sideswiped a city bus, and ended up hitting a concrete bench. The car hit hard enough for the steering wheel to give him a really bad bloody nose and split lip. By the time the cops arrived, there was blood from his nose and mouth all over the front seat area and blood from Pancho's head rolling around all over the back end of the car. Besides wrecking the car, the other big mistake that Ed made was when the cop asked whose head was in the backseat. He should have said that he had no idea, but in the heat of the moment, he said that it was Pancho Baker's head. That's when they locked him up.

At the time, I was worried about my friend, but I was also concerned for my own safety. Something had gone terribly wrong, and what made it worse is that it happened in Miami – USA. The Pancho Baker thing hit the fan at Langley, Virginia, and there were some very unhappy people running around with guns and a bad attitude. No one knew for sure who killed Baker,

3

but they were certainly trying to send a message to Ed. About four or five days later, Ed was released from the Miami jailhouse, there was never an indictment, and as far as I know, the whole thing evaporated in the midst of other more pressing news. Ed and I made a point of avoiding the Miami area for years after that. Neither of us was for sure what a head in the back of a car means, but it seemed like something you would want to avoid. I think they finally buried Pancho's head in his bowling ball bag.

Ed tended to piss off the fine folks at the CIA more than most. He talked too much. In June 1989, he disappeared for several days. He called me when he got back into town and said that he had had a small problem with the boss, but everything was okay, now. I took him at his word; but I gave him one of my long lectures about how he should learn to keep his mouth shut.

You see, the thing is, Ed had a peculiar sense of humor. We used to hang out at a place called the Formosa Café around the corner on Santa Monica Blvd. Sometimes there are a few good looking young girls who go in hoping to be discovered by a movie producer or director. Well, gee, that's what Ed was. Instead of telling them that he was a director, Crazy Ed would tell them he was an undercover secret agent. I cringed every time he pulled that stunt. The girls would invariably roll their eyes and look around the room for more promising men. He thought it was funny, because as the night would wear on, the girls would ultimately find out who he was and come back to talk to him. There were certain elements of his behavior I never understood.

We were in the midst of shooting one of his last movies when we were dispatched to a place in the Middle East. The plan was to leave on a Friday and get back the following Tuesday. I told Ed that it would be my last midnight flight out of the country for this outfit. He agreed; we were both getting too old for such foolishness. After we got there, we ended up getting lost and then the old Peugeot we were driving broke down and wouldn't

4

start. Ed and I spent almost a week freezing half to death in the mountains. We thought we were being rescued, only to find out that we had been picked up by an enemy force. They tried to get a ransom for us, but found out that no one really gave a damn whether we lived or died. Except for our Air America stint, the fine folks at Langley never kept a record of Ed and me. We were what they call, 'off the books.' Anyway, we spent another two days abandoned in a mud hut that had a steel bar blocking a very well built door. I would like to tell you that we made some daring escape. The fact is, a little boy with three goats finally came by and let us out. Ed and I were fired for being - 'productively ineffective.' I suppose they were right. We didn't get any pension or 401 or IRA or any other typical government benefits; it was just over.

Early on, Ed created La Brea Artists. I have always worked for him as a part of this company. Over the years, it evolved into and out of being a production company. We are now simply in the business of writing. There is usually a team of four or five writers. We call it gang writing. Most of our work is for television series.

Edward L. Hawke's Great American Screenplay is the last thing he ever wrote. He wrote it as a tribute to my father-in-law, Colonel Tom McKinney. It was a long friendship that began back years ago after a trip down to Maracaibo. As I recall, we went down there on some concern about the well-being of employees at a US-owned bottling company.

We didn't have reservations for a return flight and had a little trouble getting a flight back to *any* destination in the United States. We ended up making a stopover in Panama and then landed in Mexico City. The next flight we caught was one to San Antonio. By the time we arrived in San Antonio and cleared customs, we were too tired to get on another airplane to California. We checked into the Menger, a nice old hotel downtown. About the middle of the following afternoon, we wandered into the bar and that's where we met old Colonel Tom for the first time. He was a wild and crazy old coot who spent his days trying to have a good time.

Well, to make a long story a little shorter, he and an assistant district attorney and an old retired judge, they called Boots said they were going to Vegas, that night. The old man always had his Gulfstream standing by to go someplace. He asked us to go with him so we cleaned out our hotel room and headed west that night. My wife Marie used to get upset when I told stories on the old man, but as we have all grown older, we have decided that his drunkenness, womanizing, and other such shortcomings are real memories that won't hurt anyone, anymore. For two days, we were on a drunken toot with a different crew of wild women coming on duty every six hours.

After a series of hunting trips on his ranch, I met and married his oldest daughter. Ed was so fascinated with the man that he always showed up at the ranch every year to hunt. During those years, two things happened. One was that Ed heard almost every story of every wild thing that ever happened to Colonel Tom, and the other is that Ed fell in love with the old man's youngest daughter, Hanna. I guess that Ed and I almost became brothers-in-law, except that Hanna would never marry one of her daddy's drinking buddies. Ed and Hanna had an unusual relationship that lasted a very long time. I'm sorry that they never married.

During Colonel Tom's last year, Ed talked Hanna into helping the old man tell his story on a tape recorder. After Tom McKinney passed away, my brother-in-law, Jon took possession of the tapes and locked them away. Then, out of the blue, a few years ago Jon rediscovered the tapes in the back of a safe, packed them up and mailed them to Ed.

Dec. 12

Ed, - I ran across these tapes a few weeks ago.
Sorry I sat on them so long. We couldn't even find a tape

player around here to play them. The only thing I ask is
that if you decide to keep them or use them for that story
you've talked about, I would appreciate a copy of the
transcript.

  Also, Marie, Josh, and the kids are all coming to
the ranch for Christmas. There will be plenty of room on the
plane, so plan on coming along. I know Hanna would like
to see you. I think she's between fiancés!

  Jon

As it turned out, the tapes had a few things that Ed had never heard. For the most part, though, it seemed old Colonel Tom decided to withhold some of the stories he used to tell on hunting trips and other excursions with old friends. We included a few excerpts from those tapes. They mostly cover some issues that Ed either never heard or chose not to include in his screenplay.

This script was written 'long.' Most movie scripts run from 90 to 120 pages. If this project had ever made it to production our company would have revised it accordingly. One of the things you may notice is that Ed Hawke tends to write with an episodic style. That style may have been borne out of his more recent television writing. We decided to leave Your version long; our writers added in a lot of direction and instructions that would typically be left to the Director. For example, we added some song titles for background music. In some cases, we went into greater detail than usual to describe a scene where it might otherwise be left to work out on the fly.

Ed wanted to put everything he could remember in it. Anyone will tell you that the everything-philosophy is not a formula for success. Ed really didn't give a rat's ass, because everything he did in life was strictly for fun.

This story has women, cowboys, kids, horses, airplanes, two or three or four wars, a lost gold treasure (of course), a mummified body coming

7

through the wall, a few ingénues, Nazis, orphans, and illegal aliens. Along the way there are about three horses either shot or struck by lightning, and some poor dog gets run over. However, for all our friends at PETA, they will be happy to know that somebody is trampled by a bull, a bunch of folks get shot and for good measure, there's a cannibal on the loose. There are scenes from San Antonio to Paris to Libya to Disneyland and a bunch of other places. Ed's story of Colonel Tom's ranch has prostitutes, preachers, thieves, murderers, rapists, and rattlesnakes. There is something for everyone's interest; it has alcoholics, accidental suicides, and a fight or two. In the end, however, it is the story of the love of Tom McKinney for Anna Lee.

Most screenplays are read quickly. Producers, financial backers, actors, attorneys, various amateur critical parties, and a score of other readers simply read a script using all the skills they ever learned at an *ACME* speed-reading course. That's okay, because they have only a limited interest in evaluating the superficial value of the story and the quality of the dialog.

There is one person along the way who reads a screenplay, prior to production, with care and emotion. Typically, I would say the director reads a screenplay slowly, quietly, thoughtfully while engaging his entire life's experience to imagine, mentally create, and view every scene. They are usually the one person who reads the dialogue slowly and imagines *that* character, with all their emotional dimensions articulating the moment. The reason Directors become famous is because they are a part of an amazingly select assembly of artists known only to our twentieth and twenty-first century. From their imagination comes a very big picture, in motion, that can grab hold of the least of us and take us for a two-hour trip to places we could not have dreamed. If you have never read a screenplay before, I would recommend that you try to read this one as though You are the Director. There was never a wide screen high-definition picture as fantastic as the one within your own imagination.

Now, the last thing I wanted to mention is how this story might compare to others. I told Ed (after using my *ACME* speed reading skills!) that I believed his story has a plot much as *Gone with the Wind* – has a plot. You really do have to pause and ask yourself, "What was the plot of *Gone with the Wind*?" It was about ten hours long; surely, it had a plot. I remember that Ed looked over his glasses and said, "The only story ever worth telling is the one where the guy gets the girl." He said, "In this case, Malcolm McKinney got his girl, Tom McKinney got his girl, Jon McKinney got his girl, and you, Josh, you got your girl."

I started to ask Ed why he didn't include himself as one of the characters in this story. He must have disqualified himself by his own criteria. Edward L. Hawke loved Hanna McKinney.

I will miss him very much.

Josh Pinkerton

pinkerton.labrea@gmail.com

The Tapes

Transcript of recorded biography (excerpts from original)

Col. Tom McKinney

Tumbleton Ranch, Texas

                        78205

May 20

A few weeks back I went over here to a little town south of the ranch and asked the preacher about all this business of going to hell. I told him I was pretty sure that I would be goin' to hell, but just wanted to check and see what he thought about all that. I really didn't tell him about all my drinkin' and skirt chasin'. I figured he could likely read between the lines. Most of my troubles were known by most folks for miles around here anyway. He told me that the sins of my father didn't count against me. I assumed that went for my grandfathers too. So, I was glad of that. He told me that I didn't really even have to go out and do a lot of good deeds real quick like to go to heaven. But, anyway, it was at that point he and I got to talkin' about the real likelihood that I might actually see my wife Anna Lee when I get there. Well, I'll get back to that subject later. The only thing I might say is that he might just be bullshittin' me. I don't mean intentional like, but when I was sittin' in that half-assed little office of his, it dawned on me that he might not know much more than anybody else does.

May 22

As for my Pa, he was the first real rancher who ever worked the place. Up til that time everyone else just bought cows, rounded up the ones they could find and drove them to the first feedlots north. The place seemed to always have a strong foreman to make things work. The first foreman that I remember when I was a kid was a man named Jake. For some reason Pa walked out to the north barn one day pulled out a .45 and shot the man in the face. He told a couple of the boys to take him out and bury him. And they did. I think I was about nine when that happened.

Another thing that happened when I was about nine was a man came to work at the ranch who people whispered about. My Pa put him on and gave him a horse. The reason I remember him is that on a couple of occasions I remember that he was arguing with Pa about something. That was not normal when I was a kid. The only person that I ever saw argue with Pa was my Mom. She mostly always got her way. But every other asshole on the place really heeled-to when Pa spoke. So, when I saw this guy arguing with my Pa, it was odd. Then, one day the guy was gone. I heard more about him later, though. But, let me see if I can keep this recollection in order.

My Mom insisted that I go to a good school to learn to read and write and get some kind of graduation certificate. Pa seemed to think that sending me off to school would turn me into a girl. That kind of scared me, because it was hard enough around there without everyone thinking you were being turned into a girl. Anyway, my Mom got her way and sent me up to San Antonio. I think that I was twelve when I went up there. By that time, I could read, write and knew most of my numbers, but this was going to be more of a real school. I stayed with my Mom's little sister, my aunt Lucille.

Lucille's husband owned a saddle shop. Lucille sometimes got up in the middle of the night and would run through the house screaming, "It's raining, it's raining!" over and over. I don't know for sure what that was all about. During all the time I was there, almost three years, I hardly ever saw
12

Lucille's husband. I don't know where he was. He sort of never came home, except just once in awhile. I asked him once what Lucille's problem was. He shrugged and told me that everyone has their own quirks. Despite these nightly interruptions, I did good in school and was glad that I got to go. I got a diploma, even though I didn't really finish all the high school stuff. I started to tell my Pa about my diploma one day after I returned home. He stopped me in mid-sentence and told me how things worked. It was a little cruel and a little cold, but that was how he was. He said that when it comes to law, government, politics, land rights, water rights and a whole list of other stuff including high school graduation that it is always good to have an autographed picture of somebody in a position of authority, screwin' a really ugly goat. At the time, I remember I was more focused on the emphasis my Pa put on the goat being an ugly one. Later, I came to learn that Pa had a lot of bad stuff on a lot of people. Dealing in other people's weaknesses was one of the things our family did, back then.

Anyway, when I got back to the ranch, my Pa had given Ranger, my horse, to one of the hands. That was the first time I ever lashed out at the old man. He backhanded me halfway across that east corral. I landed in a pile of green horseshit with my brand new britches that my Mom bought for me in San Antonio. I was almost pissed enough to go back and fight the old man, but somehow I was kinda sure that I would come out on the short end of that scuffle.

May 27

The third, and last year that I rode regular with the hands I was about to turn nineteen, I think. Billy and a couple of the other really old timers would spend some time at night telling me about the ranch back in the old days. They talked about Grandpa Malcolm McKinney mostly because he was probably the most colorful. The darkest story was about some boys

13

from up around Austin who tried to rustle about twenty horses. When they caught up with the boys and the horses it was down near what we call the east creek. Malcolm lined up all four boys down there in the brush, pulled out a revolver, and executed every one of them. Billy said it was the most gruesome thing you ever saw in your life. The foreman, at the time, ordered some boys to get some shovels and bury them, but Malcolm said, "No, let the buzzards and critters clean it up."

Now, there was another story. Well, there were several stories about people going down to the east creek area and never coming back. In our family, taking a ride out to the east creek area is kind of like getting in a big black Cadillac with mobsters to go for a ride. This one story, Billy or none of the other guys ever told me until after Pa died. But, you remember earlier I was tellin' ya about the hand that Pa hired and I heard the two arguing. Well, it was believed that the fella was probably a half-brother to my Pa. Or, in other words, he was one of Malcolm's illegitimate kids, who showed up. That fella showed up dead down at east creek.

Billy told me that that wasn't the only bastard brother that Pa had. He said that years back there was a housemaid named Maria Consuela who got "with child" and then disappeared from the ranch. When I asked if something happened to her, Billy said that he believed that she was given some money or some land or something and left the place. The way Billy tried to tell the story; it was like Malcolm was doing something out of respect for Mary Lou. Getting the pregnant Mexican girl out of the house was supposedly some noble gesture. I found records about this event in later years.

May 28

I asked Billy how many men he thought had met their end down at the east creek. He said he estimated that it might be ten or twelve, but they
14

all pretty much deserved to be kilt. He said that old Malcolm sort of set the policy on not burying those guys, because it kept the evidence intact too long. The military got involved in investigatin' a killin'. It almost turned into a mess. There was a Captain who sat and pondered the issue of how a fella could slip, fall and hit his head on a rock and all the while have two bullet holes in his chest. I think what finally happened was that Pa knew a fella who knew someone else, who had a picture of a general screwin' a really ugly goat.

Well, let me get back on track here for awhile. When the Japs bombed Pearl Harbor in 1941, I was thirty-five. I think Pa was still less than sixty. There were a couple of reasons that I was exempt from going in the military. One, I was thirty-five. The other was that Pa had an exemption of some kind for everyone employed on his cattle ranch and he was a major supplier to the War Department.

What happened in the years preceding World War II is that I met Anna Lee. I was about twenty-five and she was seventeen. I know in this day and time that doesn't sound so good. But back then, she didn't have nothin' better to do than marry the biggest rancher in Texas and I didn't have nothin' better to do than marry the prettiest girl in Texas. So we did. Anna Lee had dark hair and she had these bluish-gray eyes. Even after fifty years of marriage, I would look across the breakfast table and see those eyes and would almost always pause to gaze a bit longer at her. It was something. She was the most beautiful girl this place ever saw.

The bad thing about me riding with the boys sometime is that we would end up in San Antonio eventually and then there would be the booze, then there were the girls. In the early days it worked out because I could usually sober up and clean up before I got home. One of the things that I didn't mention was that Anna Lee's Pa and her big sister ran a big trucking company in San Antonio. Anna Lee's sister, who I always called the tramp, was more about my age. Her name was really Emily. She took every trucker on the payroll for a ride at one time or another. I know one thing, when I would go into her office I never set my coffee or donut on her desk, because you didn't know what had been there before. I told Anna Lee, one time, that I could see bare butt cheek prints on Emily's desk. That sort of thing always pissed Anna Lee off when I would say it, so I stopped. Well, Emily, the tramp, saw me one night down at Garcia's Restaurant. Back then, Garcia's Restaurant was just a strip joint. What Emily was doing there, who knows.

Anna Lee got seriously mad at me. I told her I was just with the boys and the girls were just dancing and that was it. But she wasn't having any bit of that. So I said okay and that I was sorry and all that bullshit. The only thing I could think of was how bad I wanted to take Emily for a ride down on the east creek. She did die soon after that, but I didn't have anything to do with it. Their Pa died a few years earlier and then after Emily kicked the bucket, Anna Lee inherited the company. I have been running the outfit ever since. Having a trucking company and a ranch works well.

June 2

So, when the Japs bombed Pearl Harbor, I thought it would be good to go join the Army. Anna Lee threw a shit fit. I think what she did is went and told Pa what I was doing. It was the most humiliating thing that has ever happened before or since. And, you gotta remember I once had a horse and whore with the same name. What happened is Pa sent a couple of rough cowboys over to San Antonio with the sole purpose of getting me hogtied and brung home before I signed up. I guess he knew I would be at the Menger Hotel. The ranch had a contract for rooms with them, back then.

We had a bloody knockdown, drag out, butt kicking, scratching, biting, dumbass fight like you have never seen. By the time we were down the stairs and hit the stone floors, the police arrived. All three of us ended up beating up the cops and we almost made it out the door when ten more came
16

in. And that was the last I remember til about midnight when I woke up in jail with those clowns that Pa sent.

As it turned out, Pa seemed to have a photo of the judge screwing an ugly goat. We were all out of jail early the next morning. I signed up for the Army. Since I was so old and they thought I had a good education and some political horsepower they asked if I wanted to go into the Air Corps. I said yes and the rest is history. I flew B-24's. I was shot down three times. Later, when the Air Corps got the P-51's, I wanted to fly one of those things so bad I could taste it. Never got to fly one, though.

June 8

I came back to the ranch in 1945. Anna Lee threw a big party for me. Pa got a little lit. He stood up on a stand with the band and said that he was proud that Col. McKinney was home. What happened back during the war was they had these field promotions. While I was in Europe, I got two field promotions and ended up a Lt. Col. When I got back to the states, the Army somehow let me keep my rank. I have always wondered if Pa had something to do with that. He liked the idea of having a Col. for a son. Back in his day men carried their rank into civilian life. Nowadays they don't do that very much unless you're a general. But that night after Pa called me Col., everyone always called me Col. Tom or Col. McKinney. That is, everybody but Anna Lee. Anna Lee called me a lot of things over the years, but she never called me Col.

For some reason Pa took up kind of a hobby of breeding bucking bulls. I don't know why. He never rode bulls. None of the boys around the ranch here ever got into ridin' bulls. The funny thing about raisin' bulls for buckin' is that it is kind of like owning a racehorse. Or, like owning a racecar or sports team. You get to be a part of the event. You get special seats. People know who you are when you show up at the rodeo. That's the only thing I can figure about Pa and his bulls. I admit I always liked watchin' bull ridin'.

A lot of people don't know it, but those big old bulls sort of become domesticated. Most of them you can walk through their pens and they don't even care, so long as you feed and water them. Pa had almost a dozen good bulls. He was gettin' to be such an old fart that I was kind of afraid he was going to get hurt. One of the things that Pa would do before loading bulls for a rodeo was take a water hose and try to blast some of the shit off their ass. The problem with bulls is you get shit on your britches, then you get shit on your boots, and then you get shit on your shirt and then you get shit on your hands and before you know it, you have shit on your hat and then shit on your upper lip.

Pa was shootin' water at old Glass-Eye. Glass-Eye was the meanest damned bull I ever saw. That was one bullpen you didn't want to stroll through. After Pa hit him in the ass with the water hose, he turned and put his head right through a 2X10-fence rail. I told Pa that he needed to finish up with steel fences, but it was low priority. Well, when Glass-Eye put his head through that fence, Pa fell off the top rail right into the pen. You never saw an old man move so fast in your life. He went right back out of the pen through the hole that Glass-Eye had just made. That was one of those things that was funny enough to laugh at, but I wasn't ever sure that the old man might just kick my ass right out there in front of God and everyone. But I laughed to myself.

It was when he got back from the rodeo that he got pinned between Glass-Eye and a steel fence post. Killed the old man right there in the bullpen. Some of the boys thought we should kill the bull. I told them the bull was too valuable. One of my lawyers said that I might be opening myself up to greater liability if I used Glass-Eye on the circuit. Maybe just use him to breed. Can you imagine that? You would think that anybody who crawls on the back of a buckin' bull might expect somethin' bad to happen. I

18

know I would. I know Pa should have expected bad things. This bull business turned out to be more profitable than I thought. I guess when I "check out" that business will probably get sold out. It takes too much attention. My boy isn't that interested in such stuff.

The last thing I wanted to finally get to was Anna Lee. Back, maybe ten years ago I bought a jet. The damned thing was so fast and slippery that I finally traded it off. Instead I bought what they call a King Air. It's comfortable and for a long time there I was flying it. I mean, I had a pilot, but I flew it. It flew a lot easier than an old B-24 and it is a hell of a lot nicer. The good thing was that I could slow down, drop down low and fly all over the ranch. The bad thing that happened with the King Air was how I used it one time. Me and some of the boys were down at McAllen one night. Instead of calling for the plane to come get us to go home that night, we decided we would drive back late. We had to come back that night so that I could get to a meeting at the ranch around ten the next morning. Well, we went over to a place across the border in Reynosa, called Boy's Town. I'm sorry to say we got stinkin', shit-faced, messed up.

When you drive into the Boy's Town area the cops are standing at a gate and take a dollar. Inside the area is a little downtown area with nothing but strip joints and bars. After a bunch of that crappy Mexican beer, I remember throwing up on the sidewalk. One of the cops fined me twenty bucks. The stupidest thing is we went back in. Now, I'll tell you the truth. That night all we did was drink that shitty Mexican beer and we let the girls crawl all over us. But, as God is my witness, I swear that's it. Well, it kept getting later and later until somebody said, "Hey, boss, we can't make it back to the ranch by ten in the morning."

I told one of the boys to call the ranch and have 'em send the King Air to McAllen. Let me tell ya, making a long distance phone call on a Mexican pay phone in a whorehouse is not as easy as you might think. There isn't much that I remember about any of that trip til I got back to the ranch and walked into the bedroom. Anna Lee's beautiful eyes cut a hole straight through me. The very instant she said that I had been with women I could instantly smell that smell. That perfume and B.O. and whatever else mixed with cigarette smoke. I stunk like a stripper. Even my hair had that perfumy, tittie smell. Back in the old days I could have been cleaned up before going home. But with an airplane, lickety split and I'm standing face to face with Anna Lee.

I went down stairs and closed the deal. I remember it was two-point-four million dollars. I'm seventy-five years old and I swear if there was one thing I would do different in my life it would have been to miss that meeting that morning. Now, I know what you're thinking. You're saying to yourself that maybe I shouldn't have gone to the girly joints in the first place. Well, that kind of goes without saying doesn't it.

When I got back upstairs, Anna Lee had three bags packed and her maids were crying and about to carry them down to the car. Well, it didn't get much better. When she got down to the Cadillac, she got in the back seat and could smell that stripper smell where I laid across the seat when we were driving back from the airstrip. So, she had everything unloaded and they were reloading into the Lincoln. She was calling me all kinds of names. You could feel the whole ranch was hunkering down for the storm. I did finally get her calmed down a little. The problem was she wouldn't come back in the house. So, we had this three-ring show going out in front of the main house with every hired hand from here to yonder watching their big boss get his ass roasted by a hundred-fifteen pound woman. I never looked so pussy-whipped in my life.

I guess I can abbreviate this a little and just say that in the end she stood there in front of everybody and said that if I ever come home from a whorehouse again she was going to meet me with a shotgun and kill my sorry worthless ass.

The AA had these twelve steps. Most people will tell you that the hardest part is you have to make a list of everybody you might have pissed off when you were lit and go around and apologize. I had a hell of a list. The first one was Andy Wyatt. He was one of my oldest friends. I went over to see him at his place. He has a nice big spread with a lot of grass up around his main house. I told him that I was sorry I screwed him out of a four million dollar gas well deal. To my surprise, he told me that wasn't the reason he was pissed at me. He said that was just business and that he was the one who screwed me out of a two million dollar truck deal. I thought that was pretty low that that sonofabitch would do that and then not even tell me. In fact, it made me a little mad. But before I could say anything he said that he was mad because I shot his huntin' dog. I told him that I didn't shoot his damned dog. I told him I ran over the mut with the pickup. I thought it was about time that I tell him that the stupid dog wasn't worth a shit anyway. All he ever did was scare 'em up and chase 'em off faster than you could get there or get a round off. That was when Andy started getting really rude. He told me that maybe if I learned how to shoot I wouldn't need a slow huntin' dog.

Well, after that Andy called me out. Then I told him he wasn't callin' me out, cause I was callin' him out. Anyway, we were out on his front porch and he pushed me, then I pushed him and then we were fightin' on the front yard. Old Andy was wheezin' like something was the matter. I think he's got the emphysema or something and I figured he was gonna have a heart attack. Then, about when I think Andy is gonna throw in the towel, because I am whippin' his ass with one arm tied behind me, his wife Rose turns the hose on us. Now, I was sayin' that their yard is really nice. Well, years back Andy built a standpipe up by the house for water pressure. When she hit me in the face, it was like a fire hose. So, anyway, after that, I wouldn't apologize to that wheezin' asshole, if he paid me. The sad part is that he's still one of my best friends.

June 17

The big deal to me now, is that preacher over there. Wouldn't it be something if I could see Anna Lee again. One of the things he said was that I just needed to believe and behave. Well, I don't drink much or whore around anymore. I regret how much time I wasted out doing all that foolishness when all the while Anna Lee was here at the ranch. I'm really trying to behave, but it kind of reminds me of when I was doing those alcyholic twelve steps.

My boy is doing good. He's married and got two little kids. He bought an office building and is running the ranch from there. It seems goofy to me, but he doesn't want to raise the kids out here. The ranch is now running trucks, gas wells, feed lots, cows, and a bunch of other stuff. But the thing that really gets me, is the boy has spent a fortune fencing off close to forty-thousand acres for hunting leases. It's the most rugged part of the ranch. I would never have believed that part of the ranch could turn so much money. Hope they don't find too many bodies buried out there.

June 18

A few years back, the boy bought me a P-51 Mustang. I flew it a few times. To tell you the truth, the damned thing scares me to death. I had it over at the San Antonio airport. The FAA up at San Antonio told me I wasn't qualified to fly it. So, one afternoon after the FAA office closed I went out there and fired that sonofabitch up and flew it right off the San Antonio International Airport. I brought it out here to the airstrip on the ranch and dare any FAA asshole to set foot on one square inch of the

Tumbleton Ranch. If they do, I might give 'em a guided tour of the east creek area. Guess I will go ahead and sell the plane before I go, so the boy won't have to mess with it. A good P-51 is worth damned near two million dollars, now. I would have paid that much to get to fly one back during World War II.

The boy asked me the other day if I thought it would be all right if he converted the main house into a hunting lodge. I told him that it's his place, he can do whatever makes him grin. He said that he was planning on throwing maybe a million dollars at the place and putting up a lot of old photos and land documents. I told him there was a bunch of pictures of Federal Judges screwing ugly goats hidden around here someplace.

June 23

Hanna, I'm not sure this damned thing's workin' right. I'm not feeling too good. It's about two in the morning. I was drinkin' a little glass of Jack. I thought it might help me sleep. It reminded me of sittin' on a riverbank with Jon's wife back years ago. I remember that little gal took a big swig of my Jack Daniels and damned near choked on it. She was a wild ass kid. I'm glad her and Jon hooked up.

I worry about Marie, and Josh, and the kids out there in California.

I hope you…

END OF TAPES

FADE IN

EXT. GROUND LEVEL. VAST EMPTY TEXAS RANCH LAND. DAY.

There is stillness and a moment in perfect silence. Then, comes the haunting sound of wind. With the sound of wind, begins motion in plants and dust. The camera begins to move seemingly with the wind. The scene progresses through the following montage:

-herd of cattle and cowhands on horseback
-a remote, but sophisticated airstrip with large ramp and hangar
-the hangar has a sign: TUMBLETON RANCH
-there is a Gulfstream jet parked on the ramp
-inside an open hangar is a P-51 Mustang and behind it are
-one King Air 200 and an old Beech-18
-a ranch headquarters complex: barns, corrals and other buildings
-we move through an enormous garage with
-several antique luxury automobiles stored in the back
-(toward the front are late models): large SUV, two luxury cars,   large diesel 4W pickup, jeep, bass boat, etc.

The camera nears the large old house (circa mid 1800's) that dominates the complex. We see a beat-up old pickup parked nearby. At a distance from the front of the house is an old flat bed wagon (buckboard). The front of the house begins to fill the screen.

INT. INSIDE THE HOUSE – AN OFFICE/STUDY. DAY.

Inside the office, the scene progress along a series of photographs and other memorabilia. First, are color photos then, old black and white and sepia (brown tone) photos. Slowly around the room we view other artifacts that have been collected over a long period of time. The office is rich in natural wood, heavy light fixtures, leather furnishings, and deep rich, masculine colors. The scene continues.

                    COL TOM MCKINNEY
                    (An older voice) (V.O.)
My name is Col. Tom McKinney. I own the Tumbleton
Ranch. I was born in the main house, on December 8, 1916.
And now, at the age of seventy-five the doctors in San
Antonio, tell me that these are the last days of my life. Me
and my wife, Anna Lee and our three children, Marie, Jon
and Hanna will probably be the last of our family to live full-
time on this place. Seems all the kids are moving into town.
This part of Texas has been in our family for about one-
hundred-sixty years. Most of what I know about the ranch's
history I learned from men and women who worked the
place.

(pause)I thought it might be good to make a record of all I
know about the Tumbleton Ranch and the people who lived
and worked here. To begin, I must say that I appreciate that
God let me take care of this part of his world, for a little
while.

FADE TO BLACK

SUPERIMPOSITION

March, 1836

We hear the rumble of a distant thunderstorm. After a moment the screen flashes with LIGHTNING and we hear the THUNDER.

EXT. BROAD HORIZON. DOMINATED BY A DISTANT, LARGE THUNDERSTORM. DAY.

                                        CUT TO:

EXT. UNDER THE EDGE OF THE STORM. DARK-DAY.

There is a young MEXICAN SOLDIER on horseback. He is riding hard and fast. His face shows intense determination. He is noticeably "out of uniform," not wearing a hat and his uniform jacket is open and flying in the wind. We continue watching him ride as the rain begins to hit.

He comes upon a shallow ravine where he is forced to slow. From a side angle we see the horse making its way down the ravine. Then from the other side of the ravine and from a distance we watch to see the horse and rider COMING UP to the top edge toward us. Just as the horse reaches the top of the ravine (they are almost silhouetted) there is a SHOCKING BOLT OF LIGHTNING AND SIMULTANEOUS THUNDER. The lightning bolt has a tremendous diameter and strikes the MEXICAN SOLDIER and envelopes the horse in an electrical haze. The horse and soldier are both thrown backward into the ravine, disappearing from our view.

EXT. HIGH GROUND – OVERLOOKING VAST MEXICAN TROOP MOVEMENT. DAY.

There are three men. The first man is GEORGE TUMBLETON, the ranch owner. He is a tough man in his forties, with a three, four-day stubble of beard. Dust is caked on his face and powders his clothing. The other men, BOWERS AND RUSSELL are younger, lean, and hungry. Behind the men, in the far b.g. we observe the thunderstorm and occasionally hear it's rumble. We are able to see (reverse) a large number of Mexican troops on the move in the distance and below our elevation.

> Cont. COL. TOM MCKINNEY (V.O.)
> There's one thing about our family. During the first century
> out here, none of my ancestors made a habit of volunteering
> for military service. In 1836, the Texans were fighting for
> independence from Mexico. My great, great, grandpa
> George Tumbleton didn't seem to be too involved in wanting
> to fight in any wars. He was mostly interested in doing
> whatever he had to do to hang on to this land. Back then, it
> was about a quarter million acres. (Pause) As the story goes,
> George Tumbleton only did one thing having to do with the
> Mexican War. It seems he and two of his hired hands were
> out on the west mesa.......(fade)

> RUSSELL
> Mr. Tumbleton, those are Mexican troops. You can see the
> silver shine on their uniforms and saddles. Look.

BOWERS

They're headed north.

GEORGE TUMBLETON

Yeah, they're headed for San Antonio. (He pauses, scratches his chin) What d'ya spose they have goin' on up there?

RUSSELL

Boss, how bout if I ride on to San Antonio tonight. We ought to tell the Texians about those troops.

GEORGE TUMBLETON

(Thoughtfully) First let's see if we can come up with some kind of count on how many we're talkin' about.

RUSSELL

There are so damned many. How would you ever estimate the number? I never seen so many Mexicans in my whole life.

BOWERS

Me neither.

GEORGE TUMBLETON

There's thousands. Maybe three or maybe even four thousand of 'em. I don't know who they're goin' to visit in San Antonio, but it don't look like a friendly visit.

RUSSELL

Should we do somethin'?

George looks critically at the young man.

GEORGE TUMBLETON

Yeah, Russell. Maybe I could just ride down there and tell that Mexican General to get the hell off my land and go back to Mexico.

RUSSELL

I just meant, that me or Bowers could warn those Texians in San Antonio that the Mexicans are comin' and they are about to get their asses stomped. Maybe they might want to saddle up and get out, while the gettin' is good.

GEORGE TUMBLETON
If you think those Texian revolters are going to back down, you're as crazy as they are.

RUSSELL
But they couldn't be expectin' nothin' like that comin' their way. If I rode on ahead to San Antonio, I could at least tell 'em what we seen.

George Tumbleton considers the suggestion. Then he looks at the RUSSELL.

GEORGE TUMBLETON
Well, I wouldn't want it said that I didn't do my part for this cause.

He pauses and looks around. Then looks back at the RUSSELL.

Cont. GEORGE TUMBLETON
Ride on to San Antonio and find whoever is in charge. When you find 'em, tell 'em we seen almost four thousand Mexican troops.

George then pauses with a stern look and continues

Cont. GEORGE TUMBLETON
As soon as that bit of information comes out of your mouth, you get back on that horse and high-tail it straight back to the ranch. No girls, no drinkin', no nothin'. You understand? Straight back to the ranch. Whatever is goin' on in San Antonio, you don't want to have any part of. I mean it.

RUSSELL
Yes sir.

RUSSELL jumps on his horse and rides hard toward San Antonio. As the horse rides away:

COL. TOM MCKINNEY (V.O.)
That was about the long and the short of my family's involvement in the revolt against the Mexicans. By the time the information got to San Antonio, they already knew the Mexican Army was coming. And that rider that my great

grandpa Tumbleton sent to San Antonio? Well, they say that he fell in love with a beautiful senorita that night and was never seen again.

EXT. RAVINE WHERE THE SOLDIER WAS HIT BY LIGHTNING. DAY.

GEORGE TUMBLETON AND BOWERS are riding very slowly THROUGH the ravine, when they come upon the dead MEXICAN SOLDIER and his horse. The two men ride up closer and cautiously. BOWERS gets off his horse and walks up to the soldier. BOWERS kneels beside the body.

                    BOWERS
          This boy is a mess, Mr. Tumbleton.

GEORGE TUMBLETON dismounts and appears to see something of interest near the dead horse. He walks nearer the horse and kicks one of two large linen bags. It is full of gold coins and RATTLES. Both bags have fallen apart.

                    BOWERS(Turning)
          That sounds interesting, boss.

Both men gather at the bags. GEORGE TUMBLETON kneels down and opens the bag to discover that it is filled with gold coins.

                    GEORGE TUMBLETON
          Bowers, I think we found ourselves a thief. This boy has
          gone and stolen gold from the Mexican army.

                    BOWERS
          You think God struck him dead, for stealin', Mr.
          Tumbleton?

GEORGE TUMBLETON looks up at BOWERS thoughtfully. He gazes at him.

                    BOWERS
          What is it, Boss? You look kinda funny like.

                    GEORGE TUMBLETON

(Hard, tough look) Oh. Oh, nothin'. Guess I was just kind of sizin' up the situation we found here. (With an intensity and seriousness) So, what do you think about this, BOWERS?

BOWERS
Well, since you ask, Mr. Tumbleton. I was just thinkin. I suppose that's yours. Is that what you're thinkin'?

GEORGE TUMBLETON
Why? What are you thinkin'?

BOWERS
You know, Mr. Tumbleton. You know, if I had maybe two handfuls of that gold. Well, yeah, if maybe I just had two handfuls of that, you would still be rich and I would be rich enough to go back and marry my girl.

GEORGE TUMBLETON again assesses the site. He looks back at BOWERS.

GEORGE TUMBLETON
I'm afraid, Bowers, I'm goin to have to make you a better deal than that. Considering the only thing we have that's substantial enough to carry that much weight is our leather bags, you're just going to have to take about seventy or so pounds, yourself, Bowers.

BOWERS (Smiling)
You got a deal, boss.

The men start loading their loot.

GEORGE TUMBLETON
So, your girl in Kentucky? Her name is what? Bonnie Lee?

BOWERS
Bonnie May. Sweetest girl you ever met.

GEORGE TUMBLETON
You think she's still waitin' for ya?

BOWERS
Yes sir. No doubt about it.

GEORGE TUMBLETON
Well, Bonnie May is gonna get her a rich boy. That is,
you're gonna be rich if you don't lose this somewhere
between here and Kentucky.

BOWERS
Don't you worry about that, boss. I'm gonna head north til
I'm well clear of all the Mex'can troops. Maybe ride a day
or so north, then cut back east.

The two men load all their gold and begin to mount.

GEORGE TUMBLETON
Bowers, you be careful, boy.

BOWERS
Yes sir. And, thanks, boss. You know my life will never be
the same after today.

GEORGE TUMBLETON
Well, give Bonnie May a big slobbery one for me.

BOWERS nods and rides off.

EXT. OUTSIDE VIEW OF THE RANCH HOUSE AND SURROUNDING
AREA. DAY.

SUPERIMPOSITION

1859

Cont. COL. TOM MCKINNEY (V.O.)
After George Tumbleton died, his son Sam took over the
ranch. Sam was a good man with a short temper. He had a
wife Ellen and they had a daughter, Mary Lou. Now, in late
1850's and maybe about 1860, Mary Lou was eighteen years
old and didn't have any prospects of a husband because she
was what you might call a homely girl.

As Col. McKinney's voice fades, we see the scene narrow to the porch of the
old ranch house. On the porch is SAM TUMBLETON leaning against a
wooden pillar peering at something at a distance. He lights a slim cigar. His
daughter, MARY LOU is sitting in a porch swing fanning herself. Mary Lou
is a chubby girl with plain and unremarkable features. She is generally "a

bit" unattractive, however, Mary Lou has no particularly abhorrent characteristics. She is just very plain and noticeably overweight. Mary Lou is a very sweet, innocent and shy young lady.

MARY LOU

What is it Poppa?

SAM

Looks like somebody ridin' in.

EXT. – ROAD UP TO THE MAIN HOUSE – LONE RIDER. DAY.

A very young man (MALCOLM MCKINNEY) on horseback rides slowly up to the ranch house. He has a very rough, rugged, and ragged appearance. He is lean and appears to be a vagrant saddle tramp. He rides up close to the front porch.

MALCOLM MCKINNEY

Howdy, Sir.

Then Malcolm turns to Mary Lou.

MALCOLM MCKINNEY(smiling)

Howdy, Ma'am

Sam looks at the man un-approvingly.

SAM TUMBLETON

You're on the Tumbleton place. I'm Sam Tumbleton. You got business here?

MALCOLM MCKINNEY

Well, Sir. My name is Malcolm McKinney. I heard around that you might be hirin' cow hands. I been around cows all my life and figgered maybe you might have some work for a honest hard workin' man like myself.

As he finished speaking, he again looks at MARY LOU and smiles at her. We see a disapproving look from SAM.

SAM TUMBLETON

What'd you say your name was again?

MALCOLM MCKINNEY

Well, my name is MALCOLM MCKINNEY. Thought I
might start workin' my way farther west.

Again, MALCOLM MCKINNEY turns and smiles at MARY LOU. Mary
Lou does not smile back and is a little surprised that this man is paying such
attention to her.

> SAM TUMBLETON
> Mary Lou, go in the house.

> MARY LOU
> Yes, Poppa.

Mary Lou goes inside and the screen door bangs shut. Again, Sam looks
critically at Malcolm.

> SAM TUMBLETON
> Well, my name is Sam Tumbleton. Go over to the north barn
> over there and tell Jim I told you to be signed on. He'll take
> care of your wages and such.

> MALCOLM MCKINNEY
> Thank you kindly Mr. Tumbleton. I'll make you a good
> hand.

Malcolm starts to ride away, when he is stopped.

> SAM TUMBLETON
> Mr. McKinney! A couple of other things. If you're on the
> run from the law; me or my foreman will turn you in for
> nickel. And, one other thing. Don't come around the main
> house. None of the boys have any business up here at the
> house.

> MALCOLM MCKINNEY
> I understand, Mr. Tumbleton. You won't have no trouble
> out of me.

Malcolm reigns his horse gently away toward the north barn.

INT. - MARY LOU'S UPSTAIRS BEDROOM – FRONT OF HOUSE.
DAY.

We see Mary Lou staring through a slightly pulled-back curtain. She has an intense, curious and disturbed look as she watches MALCOLM MCKINNEY ride toward the barn.

EXT.– AREA BETWEEN THE MAIN HOUSE AND NORTH BARN – VIEWED FROM MARY LOU'S BEDROOM WINDOW. DAY.

We see the saddle tramp, MALCOLM MCKINNEY ride slowly toward the barn.

INT. – LIVING ROOM OF MAIN HOUSE. EVENING.

Sam's wife ELLEN is sitting in a chair working with her hands (sewing, knitting, etc). SAM is standing at a counter or bar in the room pouring whiskey into a heavy tumbler. He picks up the glass, studies it for a moment, then sets it down. Sam then pulls out a slim cigar and thoughtfully lights it. He takes a puff of the cigar, then a sip of the whiskey. Sam stares at a PAINTING of his daughter, MARY LOU. After a while, he grimaces -ever so slightly.

                    ELLEN
          What is it Sam?

                    SAM
          What's what?

                    ELLEN
          There's something on your mind, Sam. What's going on? Is
          it important?

                    SAM
          Oh, no. It's not. I. I was just. Well, I just been thinkin'
          about Mary Lou.

When Sam mentions Mary Lou, Ellen looks up with the immediate concern of a loving mother.

                    ELLEN
          What about Mary Lou?

INT. - HALLWAY OUTSIDE THE LIVING ROOM. EVENING.

We see MARY LOU as she hears her father say her name. When she hears the conversation, she quietly moves closer to the door to hear the conversation.

                    SAM
        Ellen, it looks like Mary Lou may be the sole heir to this
        place when you and me are gone.

                    ELLEN
        So?

                    SAM
        Well, I mean, we need to get her married one of these days.

                    ELLEN
        What are you gettin' at, Sam? Mary Lou is going to marry
        some nice neighbor boy.

                    SAM
        I was thinkin' maybe we oughta get that goin' pretty soon.

                    ELLEN
        Well, she's about old enough, I suppose.

                    SAM
        All of our neighbors around here have boys who are gonna
        be real prize bulls. They are gonna have a good spread of
        land and be able to pick 'em out any kinda girl they want.

                    ELLEN
        Sam. Don't you say what I think you're about to say.

                    SAM
        I'm just sayin'. Well, you may not have noticed it, but Mary
        Lou ain't a pretty girl like some around here.

As Sam speaks the scene is switched back between Mary Lou and her father.

                  Cont. SAM
        I happen to know what boys like when they see a girl. Mary
        Lou ain't got a real pretty face like some. She's kinda plain.
        Mary Lou is carrying a bit too much fat on her, too. She just
        isn't goin to be the first girl one of the neighborin' ranch
        boys is…. (interrupted)

ELLEN

Stop it!

INT. - HALLWAY OUTSIDE THE LIVING ROOM. EVENING.

Mary Lou is almost at tears hearing her father's critique.

SAM

Ellen, what I was goin to say was.

ELLEN

I don't want to hear any more of your mean talk.

SAM

Listen to me. What I was goin to say is that we just need to
get to work getting' her hitched up.
(Long pause) I just don't want... (he fades off).

Ellen stands up and walks toward him. She leans against him, lovingly.

ELLEN

I appreciate you carin' about what happens to Mary Lou.
But, I will not stand you talkin' bad about that little girl.

SAM

Well, I didn't mean to talk bad about her. I just meant that
the boys may not be knockin' down the doors around here to
marry her.

ELLEN

Maybe we'll have a party. We'll invite everybody from
miles around.

We see Mary Lou turn, run up the stairs to her bedroom and fall into bed.
She cries.

INT. – RANCH MAIN ROOM. PARTY SCENE. EVENING.

A piano is playing while people mix and mingle. We see Mary Lou dressed
flamboyantly. She is holding hands with another girl (MILLIE) and they are
laughing. It is apparent that the two are very good friends. We see a very
handsome young man (MICHAEL) walk up to the two girls. When he gets
to them, both girls look up and smile fully and genuinely. He returns their

smiles very kindly. With some hesitation and a hint of initial stammering he says

MICHAEL

Hi, Mary Lou.

MARY LOU

Hi, Michael.

MICHAEL

Hi, Millie.

MILLIE

Hi, Michael.

Both girls giggle.

MICHAEL

Uh. Millie. (He stammers)Millie, would you like to go to the punch bowl with me.

MILLIE

Sure.

MILLIE jumps up and grabs MICHAEL'S hand and whisks him away.

MARY LOU has a pathetic smile as she is left alone.

The scene continues around the room to SAM who is talking to a fellow rancher.

SAM

Willie, I got about a quarter million acres here. You know, the thing I worry about is the same thing I know you think about Is our kids goin' to be able to take care of the place as good as we did?

WILLIE

Yeah, you're right, Sam. I do think about that. Of course, I got three boys. One of 'em ought to be able to get it right. (he laughs)

SAM

I guess it would really be somethin' if one of your boys married Mary Lou. That would make your place and mine one of the biggest spreads ever known in these parts.

Willie, looks like he is thinking the idea over.

                    WILLIE
Where is little Mary Lou, anyhow?

                    SAM
There she is, over there. Maybe, you want to introduce your youngest to Mary Lou.

WILLIE sees MARY LOU. He, ever so slightly, recoils.

                    WILLIE
Sure. Sure. Sam.

WILLIE disappears. SAM sighs and looks around the room.

EXT. - OUT ON THE RANCH LAND. MEN BRANDING CATTLE. DAY.

There is a large herd of cattle with a number of men on horseback. As we progress around the herd we come upon approximately six men who are in the process of branding calves. The foreman, JIM, stands up and looks around. He speaks vaguely to those closest to him.

                    JIM
We need those other irons, or we'll be out here til Christmas.

Again, he looks around, then yells out.

                    JIM
McKinney! (He gets McKinney's attention) McKinney, come here!

MALCOLM MCKINNEY nods and rides over to JIM, the foreman.

                    JIM
We need some more irons. They're hangin' on the east wall of the north barn. Ride over there and pick 'em up. There should be, well, at least two. There may be three. Bring all of 'em back. We're gonna get this finished up as quick as we can this afternoon.

MCKINNEY nods.

                    MCKINNEY
     It'll take me about an hour.

                      JIM
     Then git ridin'.

INT. BARN. DAY.

MARY LOU is has a small basket and is collecting eggs. She is absent
mindedly humming an unidentifiable tune. For awhile she seems very
contented with this simple chore. However, as we watch her, we see that she
becomes uncomfortable realizing that someone else is behind her. She stops.
Considers a sound that she has heard, then turns around.

We see, MALCOLM MCKINNEY standing inside the barn and centered in
the large doors as the light shines behind him. The scene, at first, seems
ominous. As the camera focuses on MALCOLM, we see a pleasant and
gentle smile.

                    MALCOLM
     Howdy, Miss Mary Lou.

                    MARY LOU
     (Quietly and considered) Hello.

                    MALCOLM
      I figgered you had hired hands to pick up your eggs every
      day, Miss Mary Lou?

                    MARY LOU
      I do lots of things around here. Poppa says work is good for
      the soul. (she trails off)

MALCOLM moves closer to MARY LOU. As he moves closer to her we
see a curious discomfort in MARY LOU's demeanor.

                    MALCOLM
      Well, maybe I could help you with pickin' up the rest of
      them eggs.

                    MARY LOU

42

I don't need any help, thank you.

As MARY LOU reaches for an egg, MALCOLM simultaneously reaches for the same one and touches her hand. When he touches it, he gently grasps it and holds it for only a moment. Surprised, MARY LOU jerks her hand away and drops the egg where it breaks on the ground (floor) of the barn.

> MALCOLM
> (Gently) I'm sorry MARY LOU. That was my fault. (He pauses) I guess the touch of your hand just sort of surprised me. (He pauses again) I haven't touched nothin' that soft and gentle since I don't know when.

MARY LOU looks at him in a quizzical and alarmed way. She cannot speak.

> MALCOLM
> Are you okay, MARY LOU?

> MARY LOU
> Yes.

For an uncomfortably long time, the two gaze at one another.

> MALCOLM
> Can I ask you a question?

> MARY LOU
> What?

> MALCOLM
> Well, I better not.

MARY LOU looks away.

> MARY LOU
> I guess I better see if there are any more eggs.

MALCOLM again takes MARY LOU's hand. She is shocked and a little afraid of the man, now.

> MALCOLM
> I never touched nothin' so soft as your hand in my life, Mary Lou.

I was wonderin'. Have you ever kissed a man?

She is shocked by the question and we see in her eyes disbelief that this stranger would be so aggressive.

> MARY LOU (Awkwardly)
> Lots of times. (She looks away)

He grins and after a short pause…

> MALCOLM
> (He laughs) Who? Your Pa? (He laughs again)
> I would sure like to kiss you Mary Lou.

She cannot believe what he is saying. Her jaw drops. She drops her egg basket. She pulls her hand, but not hard enough to break, even from his gentle grip.

> Cont. MALCOLM
> You know I don't want to make you feel bad or nothin'.
> And I sure wouldn't ever kiss you if you didn't want me to.
> But, sometime every girl just needs to be kissed.

She looks back at him curiously.

> Cont. MALCOLM
> I kissed lots of girls. None of 'em ever said I kissed bad. If
> you never been kissed by a man, you must kind of wonder
> what it's like, don't you?

She continues to look at him, but will not speak. We then see a tremble in her bottom lip. It is hard to tell if she is frightened or strangely excited.

> Cont. MALCOLM
> You want me to tell you a secret about kissin'?

She is now visibly shaken and is becoming wide-eyed.

> Cont. MALCOLM
> A girl in Virginia, who kissed lots of people told me this
> secret and I didn't know it, but I think it's true. (He pauses
> and refocuses on her) She said when a man and a woman
> kiss that they both know if the one they kissed liked it. She

said if you kiss somebody and you like it, then they liked it, too. She said if you kiss somebody and you don't like it, then they don't like it either.

You know what that means, Miss Mary Lou?

She shakes her head in the negative, while staring straight into his eyes.

                    Cont. MALCOLM
          Well, it means if you like kissin' me, then I like kissin' you.
          But once you kiss me and you think you didn't like it, then it
          means that I didn't like it neither. Do you believe that?

She ever so slightly shrugs, unknowingly.

                    Cont. MALCOLM
          I was thinkin', what if I <u>didn't</u> kiss you and what if we
          woulda both liked it? That sort of seems sad, doesn't it?

                    MARY LOU
          I just remembered, my Poppa told me I wasn't supposed to
          talk to cow hands. (She tries again to pull away from him)

When MARY LOU realizes that she is still standing in the same spot, she looks straight back into his eyes and again trembles.

MALCOLM leans toward her very slowly. He stops briefly. She seems to have consented to this kiss. He gently kisses her lips, at first. We see her eyes close. Then, the kiss advances to a slightly more passionate depth. Then, it suddenly is broken.

We see MARY LOU's jaw drop. She is, again, very wide-eyed.

                    MALCOLM
          To me, that was as sweet as apple pie with all that butter and
          sugar and cinnamon. It was like warm apple pie for Sunday
          dinner. I liked it. That means you liked it, too. (He cocks
          his head slightly) You did, didn't you, girl?

This time, MARY LOU breaks away and runs out of the barn. MALCOLM is seen with a big smile.

INT. – MARY LOU's UPSTAIRS BEDROOM IN THE FRONT OF THE HOUSE. DAY.

Mary Lou is once again intently staring from behind the curtains.

EXT. – OUT OF THE NORTH BARN. DAY.

We see MALCOLM on horse back riding away to the herd.

INT. – MARY LOU's UPSTAIRS BEDROOM IN THE FRONT OF THE HOUSE. DAY.

MARY LOU stares intently at MALCOLM as he rides away. As the scene closes, MARY LOU, ever so slightly touches her tongue to her lips as though there might be a taste of her first kiss still there.

INT. – EARLY SUNDAY MORNING. MEN'S BUNK HOUSE. DAY.

JIM
MCKINNEY! Hitch up a team.

MALCOLM
What for?

JIM
What do you mean, "What for?" Cause I said to, that's what for. (He pauses) Then after you got it hitched up, you can take the wagon up to the house. The family is goin' to church.

Don't say nothin' stupid, either. Mr. Tumbleton don't take kindly to stupid talk. 'Specially on Sunday morning when Ms. Tumbleton makes him go all the way in to that church house.

EXT.– FRONT OF MAIN HOUSE. DAY.

We see MALCOLM tying off the reigns on the buckboard. As he is doing this, the family (Tumbleton, wife, daughter) comes out of the house dressed for church. SAM Tumbleton helps his wife onto the wagon. There is only one bench across the front for SAM and the two women. As MARY LOU starts to board, MALCOLM tries to help, but is brushed aside by SAM.

SAM (To MALCOLM)
We should be back around one. You can come over and pick it up, then.

46

MALCOLM makes eye contact with MARY LOU. As SAM walks around the wagon and before he boards...

MALCOLM
Well, it's a fine Sunday for goin' to church, Mr. Tumbleton.
Yes Sir. I love Sundays.

As SAM gets on board...

Cont. MALCOLM
I heard that Cookie is fixin' apple pie. I could smell that
cinnamon and butter. I always liked apple pie on Sunday.

As we see a shot of the family on the wagon, ELLEN seems intent on getting underway, SAM looks at McKinney with a dismissive eye. MARY LOU seems almost horrified by MALCOLM's reference to apple pie and his indirect communication with her. MALCOLM smiles.

INT. BARN. LATER THAT DAY.

We see MARY LOU and MALCOLM together in the barn. They are talking. MARY LOU is intent and seems angry. She has none of the shy behavior seen during their first meeting.

MARY LOU
How dare you! Don't you ever talk to me in front of my
Poppa ever again!

MALCOLM
So when did I ever talk to you in front of your Pa?

MARY LOU
This morning when you talked about that apple pie. I knew
what you were talking about, MALCOLM MCKINNEY.

MALCOLM
I was talkin' about apple pie, what are you talkin' about?

MARY LOU
You were talkin' about that kiss. I will tell you this, and I
won't tell you again, Mr. McKinney. If I ever tell my Poppa
that you kissed me, he will kill you. You may not know it,
but my Poppa has killed men before.

MALCOLM
For kissin' you?

MARY LOU
No. For all kinds of reasons. I can tell you that none of
them was as important as some cow-hand, saddle-tramp
kissin' me. So you better watch yourself!

MALCOLM
So, you would have your Pa kill me?

MARY LOU
I mean, if he finds out, he'll kill you.

MALCOLM
But you won't tell him?

MARY LOU
If you force me to, I will.

MALCOLM
And, how would I force you.

MARY LOU (Frustrated)
Like when you tried to tease me this morning about the pie.
Are you stupid, or somethin'?

At this point we see that MARY LOU is frustrated and generally upset with
her relationship with this very careless and seemingly indifferent cowboy.
She seems to huff and puff in frustration. They both stand staring at each
other. In a moment, MALCOLM takes her in his arms and kisses her
passionately. MARY LOU is overcome with passion. The kiss aggressively
progresses by both.

INT.– LIVING ROOM IN THE MAIN HOUSE. DAY.

Inside the living room, we see MARY LOU crying. She is being tended by
at least one or perhaps two maids (40ish, Hispanic). Her mother is crying.
SAM is screaming and occasionally throwing various things. The maids are
on the verge of breaking into tears. SAM has just learned that MARY LOU
is pregnant.

SAM

How in the hell does a girl get pregnant livin' a hundred
miles from no place. There ain't nobody around and she's
gonna have a baby. I wanna know dammit. I mean I wanna
know and I wanna know right the hell now; who has this girl
been with.

Ellen, if you know and you don't tell me, woman, I am
gonna really be disappointed in you darlin'. Do you know?

ELLEN
I don't know and she won't tell me, Sam.

SAM
You're tellin' me the truth, Ellen? You would tell me?

Mary Lou, tell your poppa. What boy you been with, girl?
Was it one of those boys at the party?

MARY LOU
(Bursts out in high volume of crying)

SAM recoils at the screaming and crying. The maids begin to cry. The
whole room has turned to loud crying from all the women.

SAM looks around the room, then walks over to his bar and pours a drink.
Just before he is about to take a sip, he puts the glass down and walks back
over in front of MARY LOU. He bends over and looks at her at eye level.

SAM
Just tell me one thing sweetheart. Were you with one of the
Mexican boys?

MARY LOU (crying)
Noooo.

SAM thinks he has begun to break through.

SAM
Well, baby, just tell me; it was one of the hands, wasn't it?

MARY LOU nods in the affirmative.

SAM
You can just tell me his name, can't you?

MARY LOU

No.

SAM

Why not?

MARY LOU

Because you'll kill him, Poppa! And I love him!

At this point, we see a tormented expression on SAM's face. The very idea that this girl is in love with one of his cow hands is beyond understanding.

Now, even more intently, SAM leans in close to MARY LOU. He speaks with a greater softness than we have heard thus far.

SAM

Well, baby, if you love him then I won't hurt him. But, we need to get all this straightened out. Now, don't we? So, your Ma and me just need to know who the man is you been seein'. You can tell me, can't you sweetheart?

MARY LOU

(sobbing)You promise you won't kill him, Poppa?

SAM nods slowly in the affirmative, awaiting the disclosure.

Cont. MARY LOU

Well. (She looks around) Well. (More calmly) Well.

DIRECT – CLOSE UP SHOT – FACE ONLY – SAM
Quietly, SAM repeats the name that we did not hear MARY LOU say.

SAM

Malcolm McKinney.

We see SAM stand straight up. He turns on his heel, heads straight for a gun case where he pulls out a rifle. We hear ALL OF THE WOMEN screaming.

EXT. – FRONT PORCH OF MAIN HOUSE. DAY.

SAM comes storming out of the front door of the main house. We can see the fury in his eyes and bearing. He is going to kill MALCOLM.

SAM

Malcolm McKinney!

SAM spots MALCOLM working on something up against a fence on a nearby corral. When MALCOLM hears his name, he looks up.

Cont. SAM

Meet your maker, you sumbitch!

MALCOLM

Uh-oh.

We now see SAM taking long strides out across the yard to the corral. Behind him he is followed by four screaming women. As we watch the scene progress, MALCOLM drops something and makes a run for a saddled horse. As he is running, SAM takes aim. He fires. Just as he fires the rifle, the horse that MALCOLM is running for drops dead, hit with the stray round.

SAM

Dammit! I shot the horse.

This time we see right down the sights of the rifle. The sights are perfectly aligned to the center, between MALCOLM's shoulder blades. Just as the gun goes off, MARY LOU's hand hit the barrel. We can see that MALCOLM has been shot in the hip. It is a bad wound. All of the women rush past SAM and out to the aid of MALCOLM. SAM raises the rifle with one hand and lays it back across his shoulder. He stands for a moment and watches the scene. Cow hands who were in hiding come out. MALCOLM is surrounded.

SAM turns back toward the house, walks up to the porch. As he sits down, he lights up a thin cigar. The foreman, JIM, walks up. For a moment, the two men gaze quietly at the scene where MALCOLM has been wounded. JIM looks at SAM.

JIM

(Softly) You missed him, Boss. (With emphasis) There was just that moment you coulda shot him, but that moment has past. You missed him. You cain't shoot him now. It's just too late to shoot the son of a bitch now.

JIM looks at SAM, expecting some reaction, but there is none. He looks back out to the scene, then continues softly.

Cont. JIM

If you would like, we could wait til he gets all healed up.
(Pause) We could wait til he gets all healed up and me and
some of the boys could take him for a ride down by the east
creek. He might fall off his horse, or somethin'.

After a while.

SAM

We'll think about that. Looks like MARY LOU is in love
with that steamin' worthless pile o' horse... (Pause)
Sometimes, Jim, I ain't sure I really know what goes on in
the female mind. They ain't stupid. In fact, they can get the
drop on you when you don't even see it comin'. It seems that
a woman is like a high strung horse. You can be ridin' along
and everything is just fine, then for no damned reason, at all,
they spook and jump sideways about six feet. Then all of a
sudden-like, when you thought all was fine, you find
yourself settin' on your ass in the middle of a cactus patch.

JIM

I ain't workin' for him Boss. I don't know where he's gonna
fit in around here, bein' married to the Boss's daughter, but I
ain't workin' for him.

SAM

Well, I wouldn't worry about that for awhile. I intend to be
the Boss of this place for a long time to come. Anyway, who
knows, he may die of lead poisoning, yet.

INT. – MAIN HOUSE DINING ROOM. DAY.

The large dining room table is surrounded by SAM, ELLEN, MARY LOU,
HER BABY, MALCOLM, JIM, and ANOTHER COUPLE. Everyone
around the table is eating what appears to be a holiday dinner. There is a
large turkey, partially carved, a ham and various other dishes. The table is
well decorated and it is a lavish meal. Where MALCOLM has been a
slovenly character, we now see him only slightly better groomed. In fact, his
shaggy hair looks as though it was the primary focus of his grooming, since it
is wetted down and combed. Just the same, MALCOLM still appears out of
place at this table.

MALCOLM (To SAM)

(Politely) Mr. Tumbleton, would you please pass the mashed potaters?

SAM stares at MALCOLM with disapproval as he passes the bowl of potatoes.

SAM (To MALCOLM)
McKinney, I heard that the Confederacy is lookin' for more soldiers. You ever thought about a military career?

MALCOLM
(Thoughtfully and with a mouthful of food)
I did, Sir. Yes Sir, I surely did think of a military career. But, like you know, I got a wife and boy, now. And, of course, that wound in my ass kind of makes me run slower than I should. So, I would hate to be tryin' to get away from a bunch of Union soldiers at a full limp. Best I can tell those Confederates are eatin' their horses.

COL. TOM MCKINNEY (V.O.)
And, once again, this was about the extent of my family's involvement in the business of war. It was said that the Union Army bought two cows, then stole about a hundred and twenty head. Then, the Confederates came through and stole all the cows they could find, then took the horses and most all the chickens. But, like grandpa Tumbleton would later say, "It was the least we could do for the war effort."

EXT.– STREETS OF OLD SAN ANTONIO, OUTSIDE A SALOON. DAY.

SUPERIMPOSITION

FIFTEEN YEARS LATER
(Fades to)
SAN ANTONIO, TEXAS

We hear the sounds of horse teams and street sounds in the dusty, dirty area leading up to the saloon. As the scene progresses to the saloon, we hear a piano playing and men laughing.

INT.– DARK GRITTY SALOON, MEN PLAYING POKER, BAWDY WOMEN AT THE BAR AND AT THE TABLES. DAY.

We recognize MALCOLM MCKINNEY, who has aged. He is sitting at a table playing poker with five other men. An attractive, much younger, gaudy girl is leaning up against him from behind rubbing his shoulders.

> GIRL
> Malcolm, I thought we were goin' to have some fun.

> MALCOLM
> Give me two cards.(MALCOLM tosses a couple of cards out of his hand)
>
> We're goin' to have some fun sweetie. I just got to get back a little even first.

> GIRL
> That could take all night, Malcolm.

> MALCOLM
> No, it'll be just one more hand.

> GIRL
> Well, I think I'll just wait over there at the bar with that lonesome cowboy, til you play your one-more hand.

> MALCOLM
> Four sixes, boys.

Malcolm lays out his cards and rakes in the table winnings. He stands up and looks around. He sees the girl flirting with a cowboy at the bar. MALCOLM walks over to the two.

> MALCOLM (To the cowboy)
> Get lost, hombre.

> COWBOY
> Who the hell do you think you are? I'm talkin' to the lady.

> MALCOLM
> She forgot to tell ya that she's with me.

> COWBOY
> I think she's with me, asshole.

MALCOLM viciously beats the cowboy senseless. As he backs away from the man lying on the floor, others rush in to assess his injuries. We see the girl stupefied by the overreaction and violence displayed by MALCOLM. We are surprised to see MALCOLM pull out his revolver, cock it, and aim at the man on the floor. We then see the cowboy on the floor look up and see the gun pointed at him. He seems to be mustering all his strength to raise up roll over and get out of the saloon. As he is beginning to crawl and stand up we hear him speak once more.

                    COWBOY
I don't want no more trouble. I'm leavin'. Don't shoot.

The whole room is staring at MALCOLM. MALCOLM puts the gun back into it's holster. He wipes his chin with the back of his hand. He looks at the girl.

                    MALCOLM
I thought we were gonna have some fun darlin'.

The GIRL nods.

EXT.– NEAR ONE OF THE CORRALS AT THE TUMBLETON RANCH. DAY.

We see ranch activity, including men working, riding horses, etc. We see fifteen year old, SILAS MCKINNEY (son of MALCOLM and MARY LOU) running energetically out to see his grandfather SAM TUMBLETON. He has a smile on his face and is upbeat.

                    SILAS
Hi Grandpa. Mom said you wanted to talk to me.

                    SAM
Where's your Pa?

                    SILAS (More serious)
I dunno. I thought he had to go into San Antonio for somethin', but I don't know what. Why? Do you need him?

                    SAM
It doesn't matter. Hell no, I don't need him. I never needed that worthless sonofabitch.

SILAS has an obvious hurt feeling as his grandfather, again, speaks ill of his father.

SAM looks up at the boy and seems to soften his tone.

                    SAM
What I meant, Silas, is that your Pa and me never had much
to do with each other. It don't matter none. He's always
treated you and your Mom fair. But, boy that's what I
wanted to talk to you about.

Come over here and sit down.

The two walk over to a couple of bales of hay and sit down. SAM looks
seriously at SILAS.

                    SILAS
What is it Grandpa? Is something the matter?

                    SAM
Boy, you're just about to be a full-growed man. I wanted to
tell you that I think your Mom really did a fine job raisin'
you to be an honest and respectable man. I am proud of you.

The other thing I wanted to tell you is kind of complicated,
but I want you to listen real close and understand exactly
what I am tellin' you.

                    SILAS
Okay.

                    SAM
Out here in this part of the world, we work real hard to
accumulate land to make up a ranch like this. Once we get
ahold of it, we have to be careful that it don't go scootin'
away by some stupid mistake.

SAM looks seriously at SILAS.

                    Cont. SAM
What I'm sayin' is that there is a way to make sure your
ranch really stays in your family, but it might change and be
complicated every generation or so. In our case, I talked to a
lawyer in San Antonio and also to our banker. One of the

things that people do is make sure they have a will or trust that directs the ownership straight to a family member so it can't get messed around somehow.

Do you know what I'm sayin', SILAS?

                    SILAS
Yes Sir, I think so.

                    SAM
Well, anyway. You really are a direct descendant of the oldest Tumbleton who ever owned this ranch or who ever dreamed of ownin' this place. Do you know what that means.

                    SILAS
Well, I kind of thought it meant that I might own this ranch someday when Pa gets old and passes on.

                    SAM
               (Pointedly and with Emphasis)
No. Boy. That ain't what it means at all. What I am tryin' to tell you is that You. Not your Pa. And, as hard as it might be to understand; not your Mom, either. It's you boy. You are at this time in history the sole heir to this whole place.

                    SILAS
But why wouldn't Pa or Mom have it before me?

With some hesitation SAM continues.

                    SAM
Well, son, understand. This ain't nothin' against either one of them. This is just the best legal way of makin' sure that a whole other generation keeps control of this place.

Say, for example that if this ranch went to your Mom or Pa or both, it could get really messed up if they had any problems with each other. You see what I mean.

                    SILAS
I guess. What kind of problems?

                        SAM
Just man and wife problems. You're not old enough to
worry about that, though.

But, remember this conversation. And the thing you want to
think about as you get older and when I am not around is that
you need to be careful to protect how this place is passed
down. Maybe, one of these days what you might want to do
when you got kids is (he pauses). See, you might want to
leave this ranch instead of to your kids, you might actually
leave it to one of your grandchildren which would, once
again insure that it is in the family far into the future.

SILAS nods.

                        SILAS
It's kind of a sad thing to talk about, isn't it grandpa.

                        SAM
I suppose. But, son, this is what men talk about when they
talk business. You got to always be thinkin' about the
business of ranchin'.

I don't mean nothin' bad by it, but your Pa ain't no rancher.
Never was, never will be. But, boy, you are. You're a real
cattleman. You may be the first rancher in our family who
can actually make some money on this place. You can do it.

And now that I think about it, it aint sad at all. I feel damned
good knowin' that this old ranch will be goin' to a real
rancher. A direct descendant of the oldest Tumbleton who
ever was.

                        SILAS
And, the oldest McKinney whoever was, too.

                   SAM (Weaker)
Yeah.

                COL. TOM MCKINNEY (V.O.)
My grandpa, Silas McKinney, apparently had a lot of talks
with his grandpa. All of my life I heard little bits of wisdom
that came from Grandpa Tumbleton. The reason I mention
this particular subject is because Pa and grandpa made such

a big deal of it to me. One of the most fantastic things that ever happened to the Tumbleton was regarding the very subject of who owned the place and who could buy and sell the land. It was right after great-Grandpa Tumbleton died, in the year of 1888.

EXT. – GRAVESIDE – FUNERAL GATHERING. DAY.

We see a much older MARY LOU crying at the casket of her father. However, this is the only crying in this scene and it moves by quickly. There are a number of attendees, including all of the men who work on the ranch. As the camera makes its' way around the attendees we observe only silent reverence for the passing of this man. This camera shot (of solemnity and silence) will be made similarly at other funerals for the purpose of contrasting one, last, very sad funeral.

>   ATTENDEE #1
>   (to another, whispering)
> That sorry, Malcolm McKinney, couldn't even show up for his father-in-law's funeral.

>   ATTENDEE #2
> He's probably bedded down with some whore in San Antonio.

We see twenty-five year old SILAS turn slightly to hear the attendee speaking of his father.

>   ATTENDEE #1
> You would think, out of respect for Mary Lou, he woulda showed up.

We see SILAS walk to and escort MARY LOU away.

EXT.– STREETS OF SAN ANTONIO – FRONT OF SALOON. DAY.

>   COL. TOM MCKINNEY (V.O.)
> On the very day of Sam Tumbleton's funeral, Malcolm McKinney was, as you might expect, in a San Antonio saloon playing poker. There is much made of that poker game that day. There are many who still prefer to believe that he won an additional 190,000 acres on a poker hand. It wasn't true, though. What he did do, was throw the ranch into debt for almost fifty thousand dollars.

INT.– SALOON. MEN PLAYING POKER. DAY.

We see MALCOLM sitting at a table with another man, BEN MURPHY.

> COL. MCKINNEY (V.O)
> The biggest mystery in our family was about Malcolm
> McKinney. The way the story goes, Malcolm was playing
> poker with Ben Murphy in San Antonio. For some reason
> Ben offered to sell Malcolm his 190,000 acres for about fifty
> thousand dollars. Back then, that was a lot of money. A lot
> of people don't know it, but for the first hundred years, the
> Tumbleton Ranch was land rich and cash poor. There were
> times when the ranch barely made payroll and that was when
> a lot of our men worked for a dollar a day. Anyway, there
> was supposed to be about that much gold hidden in the
> house. Great, great grandpa Tumbleton accumulated it, or at
> least that's the term that has always been used. Silas,
> grandpa Malcolm and Mary Lou supposedly knew where it
> was.

EXT. FRONT OF RANCH. DAY.

MALCOLM is riding up to the house, gets off his horse, and ties it to a
hitching post. CONSUELLA (maid) is sweeping the porch.

> Cont. COL. MCKINNEY (V.O.)
> The idea was that the gold was to never be touched. Instead,
> it would be the last resort in order to save the ranch if
> anything ever happened. The theory is that Malcolm was
> going to use that gold to buy the acreage. Ben Murphy and
> Malcolm agreed to meet at the bank at two or three that
> afternoon. Now, this is what happened. Consuella, was one
> of Mary Lou's maids and she was out on the front porch
> sweeping it off for the company that would come over after
> Grandpa Tumbleton's funeral. According to her, Malcolm
> rode up to the front of the house, tied up his horse to the
> hitchin' post and went in the house.

CONSUELA then leaves the front porch and the camera follows her to the
kitchen, where she proceeds to work.

INT. KITCHEN

Scene of CONSUELLA working.

EXT. FRONT OF RANCH. DAY.

BEN MURPHY rides up to the house.

>   Cont. COL MCKINNEY (V.O.)
> After that, she went to the kitchen to tend to other things.
> Malcolm's horse was later found, still tied up. But, Malcolm
> was no where to be found. The next morning, Ben Murphy
> rode up to the house lookin' for Malcolm. Silas, who was
> only about twenty-five at the time talked to Ben and that is
> when he found out that the land deal had been made.
>
> Well, to make a long story a little shorter, everyone looked
> for Malcolm. Then, my grandpa Silas and my great-
> grandma, Mary Lou, looked for the gold, which was
> unfortunately --missing. There were excuses that Malcolm
> probably got the gold and was robbed and probably killed.
> Why his horse was still at the house, no one could ever
> explain. In the end, my Silas was actually the sole heir to the
> ranch and he stood good for the deal Malcolm had made at
> the poker tables with Ben Murphy. The Tumbleton ranch
> was in debt for about fifty thousand dollars that it didn't
> have. Overnight, the ranch was one of the biggest in Texas.
> Mary Lou buried her father and lost her husband on the same
> day. She died about three months later. All the old people
> would say that she died of a broken heart. As for Malcolm
> McKinney, none of the folks who lived during that time
> would ever know what happened to him. The mystery of
> Malcolm's disappearance wouldn't be solved for another
> seventy years.

INT. CHURCH WEDDING SCENE

We see the adult SILAS MCKINNEY standing at the marriage altar with his
bride, CYNTHIA.

>   COL. TOM MCKINNEY (V.O.)
> It seems that shortly after that Silas got a hankerin' to be
> married. He brought home his childhood sweetheart,
> Cynthia.

INT. BEDROOM SCENE OF JAKE MCKINNEY BIRTH

A family gathering where the baby is given to the mother.

                    CONT. COL. TOM MCKINNEY (V.O.)
          As it turns out, my dear sweet grandmother and my grandpa,
          Silas didn't get married none too soon. My pa, Jake
          McKinney was born, legitimate, I might add, on April 12,
          1888. But, the family don't talk about that too much.

          My pa, Jake, grew up right here on the ranch. Lived his
          whole life here. Fact is, I can't tell that he ever went
          anyplace else but this ranch. I asked him once how he
          happened to meet my mom, Rebecca. My pa was more a
          mystery to me than about anybody I ever knew.

          Anyway, my mom Rebecca and my pa had one kid in their
          lives, and that was me.

EXT. FRONT OF RANCH

We see EIGHTEEN YEAR OLD 18YO- TOM MCKINNEY [Note For the
purposes of this sequence of scenes, there will only be one actor in his teens.
He will age only a couple of years from beginning to end of high school and
subsequent work experience; and referred to as 18YO- TOM MCKINNEY.
There will be no reference to elementary or other earlier schools.]

                    JAKE
          Tom! Tom! Come in the house. Your mom is lookin' for ya.

                    COL. TOM MCKINNEY (V.O.)
          While I was growing up, my mom, Rebecca, was very
          serious that I get a good education. When I was old enough
          for high school, she sent me to San Antonio to stay with my
          aunt Lucille.

INT. OLD HOUSE IN DOWNTOWN SAN ANTONIO. NIGHT.

We see a dark interior of an old house. All is quiet and still. The camera
moves through the hall quietly as though it is haunted.

                    Cont. COL. TOM MCKINNEY (V.O.)
          What my mom didn't tell me about aunt Lucille was that she
          had some peculiar quirks.

As the camera moves down the dark hall, aunt Lucille surprisingly appears at a bedroom door in her night gown.

> AUNT LUCILLE (Screaming at the top of her lungs)
> It's raining! It's raining! It's raining!

The screaming trails off into the dark.

> Cont. COL. TOM MCKINNEY(V.O.)
> I never did figure out what all the screaming was about.
> Don't really ever remember it raining much. Poor old aunt
> Lucille had some kind of problem. Back in those days we
> just kind of pretended that it never happened.

INT. CLASSROOM. DAY.

We see a typical 1932 class room. All the students appear bored to death. There is a very fastidiously dressed man, MR TIMMONS, teaching the class. No one is paying much attention (Which will be contrasted to a later scene). 18YO- TOM MCKINNEY is sitting about half way back in the classroom. His best friend COOP SAMSON is sitting nearby.

> MR TIMMONS
> (uniquely less than masculine timbre)
> Finally class, I have an announcement. I have been saving
> this until now, because I did not want to upset anyone. This
> is my last day as your teacher. The Dallas school system
> needs an experienced teacher very badly. I hope you
> understand how much I hate to leave you.

The going away speech tends to fade away as students sit up and listen only moderately more intently. Then his speech is interrupted by COL. MCKINNEY.

> COL. TOM MCKINNEY (V.O.)
> We never really disliked Mr. Timmons. He just had this way
> of putting you straight to sleep at around two-thirty in the
> afternoon. But what followed Mr. Timmons was something
> that none of us could have ever expected.

INT. CLASSROOM. ANOTHER DAY.

We see a very beautiful twenty-one year old female school teacher SHANNON (SHANNY) HOLLISTER. There is something about her.

Unlike MR TIMMONS, SHANNY moves about the classroom. She has grace and poise and movement that is similar to a slow and seductive dance. SHANNY smiles and knows that the boys are studying her and the girls want to be like her. SHANNY'S dress is appropriate, but it is snug enough to ensure there is no mistaking or missing her feminine attributes.

> COL. TOM MCKINNEY (V.O.)
> I swear. At that time, I had never seen anything like Shanny Hollister in my whole life.

INT. CLASSROOM. DAY.

As SHANNY is speaking, she stops and (affectionately) straightens a girl's hair and replaces the hairpin. As she continues speaking she notices that one of the boys (COOP SAMSON)is on the wrong page in his book. SHANNY tends to lightly touch various children as she moves through the class. She leans in beside COOP to flip the pages. As she leans down beside him, we see COOP lean in closer to her with his eyes closing as he seems to inhale her essence. He then turns to TOM MCKINNEY and smiles.

> Cont. COL. TOM MCKINNEY (V.O.)
> It was during that year of high school that I learned the true meaning of day-dreaming.

DREAM SEQUENCE - EXT.– SURREAL IDYLLIC POND (GREEN SCREEN GENERATED) DAY.

TOM MCKINNEY leaps from the fishing dock. He goes completely under the water. Just as his head pops up out of the water, he is face to face with SHANNY. We see her bare shoulders above the water. Both are face to face with enthusiastic and admiring smiles.

> 18YO- TOM MCKINNEY
> (Softly) Hi, Shanny.

> SHANNON
> Hi, Tommy. Tommy. Tommy?

INT. CLASSROOM. DAY.

18YO- TOM MCKINNEY comes back to the present with SHANNY leaning down in front of him.

> 18YO- TOM MCKINNEY

Sorry, I must have drifted off, Miss Hollister.

SHANNY
(Softly and almost seductively)
It's okay (She pushes back a lock of hair over his eyes and smiles). Can you read it for us?

18YO- TOM MCKINNEY
Sure (His eyes lock on hers a bit too long). (He points at the page) You mean, from here?

SHANNY (Nods - affirm)

18YO- TOM MCKINNEY
(Reading)
While Adrian was downing the old tree, a serpent came to him and said, "This is your last day on earth. It is time for me to take you away. Before I take you from your land, from your home, and from your family; tell me, Adrian, what have you learned here on earth?" Adrian looked at the serpent; swung his ax and killed it. Then Adrian said, "I have learned that opportunity cannot be long and wisely pondered."

INT. AUNT LUCILLE'S HOUSE. NIGHT.

AUNT LUCILLE (Screaming)
It's raining! It's raining! It's raining!

COL. TOM MCKINNEY (V.O.)
After awhile I actually got used to aunt Lucille and her screaming. It was a bit unnerving at first. Then, it was just before I was about to graduate from high school, I woke up in the middle of the night to something else even more odd.

INT. AUNT LUCILLE'S HOUSE. 18YO- TOM MCKINNEY'S BEDROOM. NIGHT.

18YO- TOM MCKINNEY is asleep. We hear a noise in the room. He rolls over in bed and his eyes begin to open. The moment he opens his eyes there is shock and fear. He jumps up against the headboard.

Sitting on the end of his bed is a feral young man (JACK) about the same age as Tom. JACK has a wild and fearsome look in his expression. He is grinning oddly with a hint that he might be crazy.

                    JACK
You're Tom. (He grins more vigorously with satisfaction)

                    18YO- TOM MCKINNEY
Who the hell are you?!

                    JACK
I'm your cousin. I'm your cousin, Jack.

                    18YO- TOM MCKINNEY
I don't have a cousin named Jack.

                    JACK
I live at your place. You live at my place and I live at your place.

                    18YO- TOM MCKINNEY
What are you talking about? I live at the Tumbleton Ranch. This is my aunt's house.

                    JACK
I know. This is my house. I don't live here anymore. I live at your ranch.

                    18YO- TOM MCKINNEY
If you live at my house, how come I have never seen you before?

                    JACK
Everybody is afraid of me. (He chuckles) They think I'm crazy. (False chuckle) I'm not though. (Frighteningly serious) Sometimes I stay in your barns. Sometimes I stay out with the cows. Other times I just wander through your house. There is one old cabin on your place where I stay mostly. If you ever wanna come see me, I might be there. I gotta go.

JACK jumps off the bed and through an open window and is gone.

                    AUNT LUCILLE (O.S.)

Screaming (Running down the hallway outside the door)

>   COL. TOM MCKINNEY (V.O.)
I'm not sure how much I learned in high school from
Shanny's class. The main thing I learned was how moved a
young man can be by the nearness of a beautiful woman. I
suppose that's something.

INT. CLASS ROOM. DAY.

Everyone is filing out of the class room except that 18YO- TOM
MCKINNEY has stayed behind. He is staring at SHANNY with an
intentness that implies he is nervous.

>   COL. TOM MCKINNEY (V.O.)
It was on our graduation day. Shanny had just given some of
us our graduation certificate because we weren't going to be
at the graduation ceremony. Now, mom would have liked
going to a graduation, but I just wanted out of aunt Lucille's
house so bad that I failed to mention the ceremony. The
screaming was one thing, but that visit from Jack just put me
on edge for the rest of the time I was there. Anyway, I had
my graduation certificate in my grubby little hands and
figured nobody could take it away from me. Even now, it's
hard to believe what I did.

>   SHANNY
Is there something else Tommy?

>   18YO- TOM MCKINNEY
Yes ma'am.

>   SHANNY (smiling)
What is it, Tommy? Is everything okay? You look a little
upset.

>   18YO- TOM MCKINNEY
Oh, no. I'm not. I'm not upset.

18YO- TOM MCKINNEY walks straight up to SHANNY and kisses her on
the mouth. We see SHANNY'S eyes wide open in shock as she recoils from
a hard and unaffectionate kiss.

>   SHANNY

Tom McKinney!! What in the world are you doing?!

As 18YO- TOM MCKINNEY starts to back away with a shocked look on his face, SHANNY grabs a fistful of his shirt and does not allow him to escape.

Cont. SHANNY
Don't you know that behavior like that is disrespectful.
(with emphasis) It's not nice. When you do something like
that it means that you don't think very highly of me! You
don't steal kisses from your school teacher! Is this the way
your mother and father have taught you to treat women?

18YO- TOM MCKINNEY
No ma'am, but.

SHANNY
Don't say, "but" to me! There is no, but.

18YO- TOM MCKINNEY (weakly)
I'm sorry.

SHANNY
That's it? You're sorry.

18YO- TOM MCKINNEY
Shanny, it's just…

SHANNY
(Even more shrill) Shanny?!! Since when did you start
calling me Shanny?

18YO- TOM MCKINNEY
I'm sorry, but what I meant to say Miss Hollister. Well, it's
kind of embarrassing. I don't know what to say, but Miss
Hollister you're the prettiest woman I ever saw in my life.
In the whole world I'm thinkin' there may not be as pretty a
woman anywhere.

SHANNY (releasing her hold on his shirt)
So, you kissed me because you think I am pretty? Do you
kiss all the girls that you see who are pretty?

18YO- TOM MCKINNEY

Sometimes, I guess I try to. Most of 'em let me, though.
And, they don't get mad.

SHANNY
(smiles slightly)
You know what Mr. McKinney. You are doing it all wrong.

18YO- TOM MCKINNEY
I am?

SHANNY (again
seriously, but kinder)
Yes. Tom, you don't ever have to steal kisses from the girls.
Boys and men like you are going to get all the kisses from all
the girls you ever want. You need to focus on just being
nice to the girls. Whatever you do, you need to be especially
nice to all the girls, Tom. They are all going to want you to
love them. Don't steal from them.

18YO- TOM MCKINNEY
I don't think I know what you mean.

SHANNY
I mean, don't steal kisses from the girls. Just ask them for a
kiss. Some might say no, but there will be plenty who will
say yes. (pause and softly) I want to show you something.

SHANNY again gently takes his shirt and pulls him close to her. In an
agonizingly slow and deliberate approach, she leans into him and kisses him
with a gentle, but passionately moist loving kiss.

As SHANNY pulls away, 18YO- TOM MCKINNEY is in a mild state of
confusion and stumbles backward into a stack of books that are on a desk.
The books and he fall to the floor. He begins gathering up the books and
looking back at SHANNY who is standing tall over him, gently smiling.

SHANNY
You're a handsome boy, Tom McKinney. You don't have to
steal kisses from the girls. (As he is getting up and leaving
she raises her voice)Tom McKinney, you come back and see
me after you grow up (she smiles, laughingly).

EXT. OUTSIDE SCHOOL HOUSE. DAY.

We see 18YO- TOM MCKINNEY coming out of the school with a tremendously big satisfied smile. TOM MCKINNEY'S best friend, COOP SAMSON is waiting for him. They join up and walk away.

COOP SAMSON
Where have you been, Tom. I've been waiting for ya. Schools over. You can't be the teacher's pet no more. (Laughs)

18YO- TOM MCKINNEY
Coop, I'm gonna tell ya this and you ain't gonna believe it.

COL. TOM MCKINNEY (V.O.)
High school turned out to be a good deal. As embarrassing as it was, I was always happy about that time that I kissed Shanny Hollister. I guess I was even happier about the fact that she decided to teach me a thing or two about kissin' before she let me go. I felt that kiss for the rest of my life. It was the one by which all others were ever measured.

INT. RANCH MAIN HOUSE. DINING ROOM. NIGHT.

Sitting around the evening dining room table eating dinner are 18YO- TOM MCKINNEY, JAKE, AND REBECCA. The scene is subdued by low volume discussion in a room that is lighted in an old fashioned yellow hue. The room is rich with heavy wood and furniture.

JAKE
You know your mother wanted to see you graduate.

18YO- TOM MCKINNEY (to REBECCA)
Mom, I'm sorry. But, I just couldn't stay another night in that crazy house with aunt Lucille.

JAKE
What's the matter with that woman, anyhow?

REBECCA
Oh. I think it was something that happened when we were kids. I'm afraid she's just getting worse. We might have to do something for her. If she gets worse, I suppose we could move her out here...

JAKE

Wait a damned minute.

18YO- TOM MCKINNEY
Mom. Oh, mom. You don't know what you're saying.

REBECCA
Well, I'm just afraid we need to help her.

18YO- TOM MCKINNEY
I think she's okay, except just at night. For some reason she keeps thinkin' it's rainin'. Why would she think that?

REBECCA (looking down at
her plate)
I don't know.

18YO- TOM MCKINNEY
And, another weird thing. Some wild kid came into my room one night and said he was my cousin. He said his name was Jack. What was that?

REBECCA looks up at JAKE, knowingly.

18YO- TOM MCKINNEY
He said that he lives out here on the ranch, Pa.

18YO- TOM MCKINNEY looks at his dad then to his mother.

JAKE
(gesturing slightly to change the subject)
Tom, he's just a lost boy. He ain't right in the head. I've seen him on the place, but he always just runs away. Don't talk about it anymore. It upsets your mom.(Glancing at REBECCA) (Pause, to TOM) What are you gonna do now, boy?

18YO- TOM MCKINNEY
(Wondering what this is all about, then indifferently)
I don't know.

JAKE
Well, I do. It's time for you to go to work. You been behind your momma's apron strings for long enough.

                    18YO- TOM MCKINNEY
Work? What do you mean, work?

                          JAKE
You don't know what work is? Well, you're about to find
out, boy. You're goin' to work.

                    18YO- TOM MCKINNEY
I know what work is. I just don't know what kinda work
your talkin' about.

                          JAKE
I'm talkin' about ranch work. I'm talkin' about you
becomin' a rancher.

                    18YO- TOM MCKINNEY
I know about ranchin'.

                          JAKE
You don't know your ass from a hole in the ground. You're
gonna learn ranchin' the way a McKinney learns to ranch.
Tomorrow mornin' you report to Billy and plan on ridin'
with the boys for a year or so.

                        REBECCA
A year or so?!

                          JAKE
Being a rancher is something you have to grow into. This is
a big place and it's gonna be yours. You're gonna know all
about it in a couple of years.

                    18YO- TOM MCKINNEY
                        (innocently)
Okay. It'll give me a chance to ride Ranger for awhile.

                          JAKE
Well, boy. Not so fast. I had to give that horse to one of the
hands while you were in school.

                    18YO- TOM MCKINNEY
                        (indignantly)

You gave away my horse?! You can't give away my horse. (To Rebecca) Mom, he can't give Ranger to somebody else, can he.

JAKE
Listen to me, boy. Every horse, every cow and every rattle snake and coyote on this place belongs to me. We aint got no pet horses. They're all workin' stock. You can let that be lesson one in ranchin'.

EXT. NEAR THE BARN. MORNING.

The HIRED HANDS are saddling horses and preparing for the days work. Billy is a hard, tough old foreman that doesn't take any back talk from anyone, especially hired hands. We see BILLY and 18YO- TOM MCKINNEY standing face-to-face. BILLY is staring at 18YO- TOM MCKINNEY.

BILLY (serious)
Yeah. Jake said you was coming to work with us, Tom. He said I was supposed to teach you how to be a rancher.

For awhile, the two stand looking at each other without saying anything.

18YO- TOM MCKINNEY
So, what do you want me to do? My old man gave my horse away.

BILLY continues to stand looking at him unkindly and without generous feelings.

Cont' 18YO- TOM MCKINNEY (nervously)
He said that I never really owned no horse because they all belong to him. So he just gave Ranger away.

BILLY
(After a long pause) Well, ya see. That's the first thing I hafta correct in your learnin'. The truth is, every horse and cow out here belongs to me.

18YO- TOM MCKINNEY
To you?

BILLY

Yep. Ya see, you're ole man has entrusted every horse and
cow out here to me. So, as a hired hand, you need to
remember that they all belong to me and I take their well-
bein' real damned serious.

18YO- TOM MCKINNEY
(Arrogantly) Well, he said the snakes and coyotes was his,
too.

BILLY
(Turning his head angrily for the apparent attitude) I don't
give a damn about snakes and coyotes. Are you stupid, boy?

18YO- TOM MCKINNEY looks as though he can hardly believe how he is
being treated.

(CONT.) BILLY
Throw your saddle on Eleanor, over there.

18YO- TOM MCKINNEY
Are you callin' this here saddle, right here that my grandpa
Silas bought me, my saddle? Or, does that belong to you,
too?

BILLY
Tom, you got a long way to go boy. You been your
momma's baby a long time. You better get ready to suck it
up. And, you better try real hard to remember who the hell
is in charge around here.

18YO- TOM MCKINNEY is on ELEANOR (a troubled horse). ELEANOR
begins bucking. 18YO- TOM is thrown off the horse and is lying on his
back in a state of temporary shock. We see some of the other HIRED
HANDS standing by with a snickering laugh at 18YO- TOM'S dilemma.

BILLY rides up beside him and looks down.

BILLY
I figured you and Eleanor would probably hit it off pretty
good since she's always had kind of an attitude, too. Now,
get off your ass, stop horsin' around and let's go.

We see 18YO- TOM and ELEANOR now under control and riding away
with the HIRED HANDS.

COL. TOM MCKINNEY (V.O.)
The thing about some horses is that they don't ever get
better. That first year, I had to break ole Eleanor every
morning after breakfast. That horse never wanted to go to
work in the morning. She was alright sometimes during the
day, but right after breakfast she was hell on wheels.

EXT. VARIOUS CAMPSITES. EARLY MORNING.

We see three separate clips at different sites showing 18YO- TOM trying to
mount and then riding a bucking ELEANOR. He is successful in staying in
the saddle.

INT. BAR ROOM, SALOON, WHOREHOUSE. NIGHT.

18YO- TOM is surrounded by older HIRED HANDS. All are drinking,
yelling and fondling the women. 18YO- TOM seems a little uncomfortable.
He smiles and sips a beer. As he is looking around, a BAR GIRL comes up
and puts her arms around him. 18YO- TOM smiles shyly.

BAR GIRL
Some of your friends said that you and me could have some
fun together.

18YO- TOM
Sorry, ma'am. I ain't got no money, or nothin'.

BAR GIRL
That's okay. Your friends already paid for ya.

18YO- TOM
They did? (He looks around)

BAR GIRL
Yep. Come with me. (she takes his hand)

INT. UPSTAIRS BEDROOM. NIGHT.

We see 18YO- TOM taking off his shirt. He is smiling broadly. The BAR
GIRL is lying on the bed waiting for him.

18YO- TOM
You mind if I turn this light out?

                    BAR GIRL
        Sure, if you wanna.

As the light goes out, we see him get onto the bed. She is laughing.

                    BAR GIRL
        So what's your name, cowboy?

                    18YO- TOM
        Tom. What's yours?

                    BAR GIRL
        Eleanor.

                    COL. TOM MCKINNEY (V.O.)
        Well, it was true. A few years earlier, the Tumbleton Ranch
        boys had actually named my wild ass buckin' horse after a
        very nice lady in San Antonio. That, however, did not endear
        me any more to the horse, though. After about a year of
        Eleanor - that is, Eleanor the horse, I had just about had my
        fill.

EXT. CAMPSITE. EARLY MORNING.

We see 18YO- TOM trying to get on ELEANOR. Finally, he is able to get on
the horse and then begins the bucking. He is thrown off the horse. Again, he
goes through the trouble of getting the horse to stand still long enough to get
back on. Everything looks just fine as they ride away 200 feet or so. Then
ELEANOR unexplainably bucks again, and he is thrown from the horse a
second time. 18YO- TOM appears to be furious. He pulls out his gun puts it
within a foot of the horse's head and pulls the trigger.

                    COL. TOM MCKINNEY (V.O.)
        To tell you the truth, I always felt bad about that day. I
        mean, don't get me wrong, even after all these years, I still
        have no tolerance for a bad horse, but Eleanor was the first
        and only healthy horse I ever had to shoot.

As 18YO- TOM stands over the dead horse, BILLY rides up.

                    BILLY
        You shot my horse?

That was a sorry ass horse. She dropped me in the dirt
twice, just this morning. I been askin' you for a good horse
for over a year. We got a hundred horses and you make me
ride this old sore head. I shot Eleanor and I'm glad. Now
give me a good horse, old man!

We see 18YO- TOM'S face turning red. He has tears running down his face
and he is breathing very hard.

BILLY

Give you a good horse? Give you a horse? I ain't givin'
you nothin', boy.

18YO- TOM

You hafta give me a horse, now. And, you know what
Billy? You cain't find another horse as sorry as this one to
give me. You gotta give me a better horse, you old son of a
bitch!

BILLY

First. I ain't givin you a horse, a donkey, or a saddled up
cow. You're fired, boy. Get your stuff and git out of here.

18YO- TOM

You can't fire me.

BILLY

(Stares for awhile)Tom, your old man can give you another
horse and send you back here, if he wants. He's the boss.
Because he's the boss I'll do exactly what he wants. But, in
the meantime, you're fired. Now, git.

18YO- TOM
(tearfully and angry)
How am I supposed to get back to the house?

BILLY

Shoulda thoughta that before you shot my horse. Start
walkin'. And, if you don't want me to give away that nice
saddle that your grandpa gave ya, then you better pull it off
that dead horse and take it with you.

18YO- TOM

(Very emotional)I cain't carry that thing all the way back to the house!

> BILLY
> (Riding away)Don't tell me your problems, I ain't your momma.

EXT. FRONT PORCH OF RANCH HOUSE. DAY.

JAKE (on the porch) and 18YO- TOM (bottom of steps on yard) are seen talking. 18YO- TOM has just arrived back at the house and appears dirty, hot, sweaty and exhausted.

> JAKE
> Billy fired ya?! (Falls backwards onto porch chair, laughing) Boy, you got fired off'n your own place? You gotta be the worst hand we ever had! What the hell did you do, to get Billy to fire ya?

18YO- TOM shakes his head trying to avoid the question.

> JAKE cont.
> Tell me, boy. What'd you do?

> 18YO- TOM
> (Quietly) Shot Eleanor.

> JAKE
> Shot who? (more seriously) who'd you shoot?

> 18YO- TOM
> (With more force)Eleanor. Eleanor my stupid horse.

> JAKE
> You shot your horse, Eleanor. (Pause) Yeah. (Pause) I guess I remember that old horse. So, Billy had you riding Eleanor. What the hell did you do to him to make him give you Eleanor?

> 18YO- TOM
> Well, let's see. Oh, yeah, I remember now. I showed up out at the barn over a year ago. That's what I did. He never would give me a good horse.

                        JAKE
You mean you been ridin' Eleanor for over a year?

18YO- TOM doesn't respond, he looks away skyward. JAKE lights up a
small cigar.

                        18YO- TOM
Pa. That was a sorry horse. I shouldn't have shot one of
your horses, but I been bucked all over this ranch every
morning for over a year and a man can only take so much til
he has to do something. It was either me or that sorry-assed
old horse. But the other thing is that I really don't wanna go
back out there Pa.

                        JAKE
Oh, you're goin' back alright. You don't have any choice,
son. You hafta go back.

                        18YO- TOM
(Again, almost to tears) Why? Haven't I had enough of
Billy and all this cowboy crap.

                        JAKE
Tom. This is your ranch. Technically speaking, this place
was in Trust to you even before you were born. It's yours.
You hafta keep goin' back. You hafta be the boss. Tom, you
can't just walk away from this.

                        18YO- TOM
But it's so hard. They give me the worst horse. I get the
shittiest shit details. And, they do all that just so they can
laugh behind my back at me. You don't know how hard it
is, Pa.

                        JAKE
So, you don't think I know how hard it is to be the boss's
son? Who do you think you're talkin' to, boy? (Pause)I
suppose I could bring you back up here to the house. You
could get on a big pretty horse every once in awhile and ride
around the place and give some orders. In fact, someday,
maybe that's the way you will want to do it. But if I did that
right now, Tom, the hired hands on this place would still be
laughin' behind your back. You gotta go back to work son.
You don't have a choice. The only choice you have is how

you are going to let yourself be treated by those cow hands. You gotta decide.

For awhile, JAKE and 18YO- TOM stand quietly and look around not saying anything.

> Cont. JAKE
> I guess, Tom, there is one thing I shoulda explained. Maybe the reason I didn't is that it's kinda complicated. Sometimes people say things in kind of a high and mighty way. One of the things we say is if you're gonna be the boss you gotta earn it. The truth is, Tom, you don't earn your way to bein' boss. You don't earn it. You just take it. You just take it, cause you want it more than anybody else, Tom.

Again, the two stand quietly. We see TOM look up to his father, respectfully.

> 18YO- TOM
> (with calmness, reserve and respect)Well, Sir. I would like to have my job back. And, I would appreciate if you could give me a horse.

> JAKE
> (Thoughtfully) Take mine. Take Mac. Take care of him.

> 18YO- TOM
> Really?

> COL. TOM MCKINNEY (V.O.)
> It was the kindest thing my old man ever did for me. Or, as best I could tell it was. Giving me his horse was something that changed a lot of things. When I rode back to the herd that afternoon on Jake's horse, Mac, I think everyone realized that I was there to stay.

INT. BAR ROOM. SALOON. NIGHT.

As this scene opens, we are introduced to the adult TOM MCKINNEY. At this point he is in his very early 20's. This character will eventually become approximately 60+ years of age.

Inside the bar is a rowdy crowd of drinkers and girls. The front door swings open and a band of Tumbleton HIRED HANDS led by TOM MCKINNEY comes in.

TOM MCKINNEY

(Loudly) Set 'em up, bar-keep! We're gonna do some drinkin' tonight! (He grabs a girl around the waist)And, we're gonna do some partyin' tonight!

COL. TOM MCKINNEY (V.O.)

There was a time that I mostly just drank and chased girls. Seemed for a long time that I didn't have much important to do. The work started to get easy and it was something that I didn't mind. In a way I was allowed to just stay young and have fun for a long time. One night when we were all out with one of the herds Billy and me got into a conversation that sort of began to change all that.

EXT. CAMPSITE WITH THE HERD. NIGHT.

TOM MCKINNEY AND BILLY sitting near a campfire, but removed from the others, are talking.

BILLY

Guess you been thinkin' about how your gonna fire me the first chance you get, Tom.

TOM MCKINNEY

The thought has sure as hell crossed my mind, Billy. Fact is, though, that Pa is gonna be around for a long time, it looks like. Long as he's in charge, seems you probably have a job. You sure never did me too many favors, Billy. When I needed the most help you gave me a sour horse. When all the boys were makin' fun of me, you just poured fuel on the fire. If I had been drowning you woulda run to find an anchor to throw at me. How come you treated me like that Billy?

BILLY

Guess I have been kinda hard on you. I've worked on five different ranches in my life. Two in Wyoming and three here in Texas. Every place I worked, I worked for men I respected. They always respected me. When your Pa sent you out here I just figured you were gonna hafta turn into a man I could respect, if I was ever gonna work for ya.

TOM MCKINNEY

Didn't you ever worry about what I thought about you? Did you ever worry yourself with whether I respected you? Did you think I was gonna respect you because you treated me bad year in and year out?

BILLY

I figured if I ever learned to respect you, that you would just have to respect me back. Let me tell you somethin' Mr. McKinney. I'll tell you as straight up as I ever did. If and when you ever get to be the boss of this place you're gonna wake up one mornin' and say to yourself, "I'll be damned. I got a half-million acre ranch to operate." What you're not gonna say is, "Let me go find a good drinkin' buddy or a poker partner to run the place for me." What's gonna happen is you're going to find a damned short list of men who can take care of a 440,000 acre ranch. And, when you get that short list, I'm gonna be on it, because, well, --it's a short list. And, I'll tell you who isn't on that list: Your drinkin' buddies, your huntin' pals and none of the boys you go to the whore houses with. No matter who you pick to run this place for you, he's gonna be as mean as me.

RIDER IN THE NIGHT

(Arriving on horseback in the night)Mr. McKinney. Your Pa wants you to come home tonight. It's your Mom.

COL. TOM MCKINNEY (V.O.)

I started out riding; seemed like I rode half the night. Mac stepped in a hole and broke a leg.

EXT. ALONG A CREEK BED. NIGHT.

We see TOM MCKINNEY standing over Mac with a smoking gun.

TOM MCKINNEY
(To the dead horse)
Oh, Mac. Look what you made me go and do.

JACK (ADULT) (O.S.)

Tom.

82

TOM MCKINNEY turns around in surprise. JACK is on a large horse, coming out of the darkness. He looks gigantic, ragged and homeless.

> Cont. TOM MCKINNEY
> (At a whisper) Crazy Jack. (Louder) JACK?

> JACK
> Your momma is dead, Tom.

TOM MCKINNEY stands quietly and sighs. He looks at JACK like someone he is not sure of.

> TOM MCKINNEY
> What do you want Jack?

> JACK
> Nothin'. (Intent grimness) Just thought I would tell ya.

> TOM MCKINNEY
> (Thoughtfully) Jack, I'm just gonna walk away, here. Don't need no more trouble tonight. My horse is dead, my mom is sick and I need to get back to the house. So, I'm gonna start walkin', okay?

> JACK
> You can take this horse, Tom.

> TOM MCKINNEY
> You're gonna let me have your horse?

> JACK
> My horse?! (laughs crazily) (He stops laughing and looks seriously at Tom) I'll just take another one.

TOM MCKINNEY sits up in the saddle of JACK'S horse and looks down at the crazy man. JACK now has a large silver bladed knife in one hand. TOM MCKINNEY still looks at JACK warily.

> TOM MCKINNEY
> So, what are you going to do, Jack?

> JACK

(With a quick hard, forced grin) I'm gonna dress out a hind quarter of this dead horse, Tom. (He laughs)

TOM MCKINNEY pauses for only a moment to look in wonder at JACK.

> TOM MCKINNEY (Riding
away)
Thanks for the horse, Jack.

> JACK (Yelling over his shoulder)
And thank you, cousin Tom!

> COL. TOM MCKINNEY (V.O.)
When I finally got back to the house, it was true, mother had passed. That was a strange and unusual night. It would be decades later before I would ever see Crazy JACK again. Over the years some of the hands would mention that they saw him. Some would say he had taken a horse or dressed out a calf. There were others who accused him of cannibalism. Some claimed it was all just a ghost story. I never spoke of him.

INT. RANCH MAIN ROOM. WAKE. DAY.

We see a number of persons milling around. There is food. People are dressed appropriate to having been to a funeral. There is a large well dressed man in his late 40's at the front door (MATTHEW BOWERS). He stands there for awhile, then comes in. He leans toward one of the guests and appears to have asked what is happening. As the guest explains, he nods. From across the room, TOM MCKINNEY seems to recognize the man. He casually moves toward him.

> TOM MCKINNEY
How do you do. I'm Tom McKinney. We've met haven't we?

> MATTHEW BOWERS
Yes sir, Mr. McKinney. Met you in San Antonio when you all brought your last herd to the feed lots. I'm Matthew Bowers; Bowers Trucking company. I had an appointment with your father, but that was before I found out about this. I am so sorry. I would like to pay my respects and then I'll just leave. Maybe we can get together later.

TOM MCKINNEY

That would probably be good. We talked about trucking the cows to Fort Worth and Kansas City.

MATTHEW BOWERS

Yes sir. Maybe, when you get time you or your Pa might want to just come see me in San Antonio. I sure don't want to intrude any more.

TOM MCKINNEY

Pa wasn't too anxious to put his cows on your trucks, was he?

MATTHEW BOWERS

Actually, no. But, I can make you a lot of money. I can deliver fat cows anywhere in the country in two to three days. (Hesitantly, he stares at Tom McKinney) Maybe you might want to come in and visit. Here is my card.

TOM MCKINNEY

Thank you. If you are in next week, I'll be in San Antonio. Will that be okay?

MATTHEW BOWERS

Sure.

COOP SAMSON walks up to TOM MCKINNEY.

COOP SAMSON

Tom. I am really sorry about your mom. She was always good to me.

TOM MCKINNEY

What have you been up to, Coop? I haven't heard much out of you in a long time.

COOP SAMSON

Started law school. Me and Sandy are gettin' married. You have to be my best man, Tom.

TOM MCKINNEY

Sure, That mostly just means drinkin' and playin' with the bride's maids, right?

COOP SAMSON
I think that's what it means.

EXT. OFFICE BUILDING. SIGN, "BOWERS TRUCKING CO." DAY.

INT. SMALL SHABBY OFFICE LOBBY. DAY.

At a desk in the front office is a woman in her late 20's or early 30's who is attractive, but hard and tough in appearance and in demeanor. EMILY BOWERS is MATTHEW BOWER'S (older of two) daughter(s).

EMILY BOWERS
Hey, stud hoss, ya here lookin' for a job?

TOM MCKINNEY
(Smiling) No ma'am. I'm Tom McKinney. (Pause)With the Tumbleton Ranch. S'pose to see Mr. Bowers about doing some cattle shipping for us.

EMILY BOWERS
Oh, sure. He's here. Hang loose for a minute I'll get him. (Picks up a phone)Hey, Dad, there's a cowboy from the Tumbleton place out here to see ya. ...Okay. (To Tom McKinney)He'll be here in minute, have a seat, sweetie.

INT. MATTHEW BOWERS PRIVATE OFFICE.

MATTHEW BOWERS
Well, thank you Mr. McKinney. I know you're gonna be happy with how this works. If we can load those cows on Monday, I will have them in Kansas City on Wednesday for sure. When you figure that you will be pickin' up ten cents a pound on fatter cows and not having to run in another twenty hired hands, your father is going to really see the benefit.

TOM MCKINNEY
Of course, if anything goes wrong, you know he'll skin both of us.

MATTHEW BOWERS
Let me assure you this is the beginning of a long and profitable relationship. I've been in this business since I was a kid. I was driving a truck for a company in Louisville, Kentucky up until about five years ago. But, when me and

my daughters came to Texas we found out how bad
everybody needed a good trucking company. We're the best,
Mr. McKinney. (He picks up a phone) Anna Lee, bring me
the standard agreement forms, baby.

TOM MCKINNEY
You know, Mr. Bowers, I don't really have the authority to
sign anything for the ranch.

MATTHEW BOWERS
I understand. But your cows will be insured, and if we have
to make a claim, I'm sure your pa won't dispute your
signature authority. So I just want every detail covered.

ANNA LEE, the younger daughter (17-18 yr.old), brings the papers in. The
moment she enters the room, TOM MCKINNEY'S eyes lock onto her. She
is a terrifically delicate and beautiful girl.

MATTHEW BOWERS
Tom, this is my youngest daughter, Anna Lee.

ANNA LEE smiles at TOM. He stands up, smiles and shakes her hand.

INT. RESTAURANT. DAY.

ANNA LEE is sitting across the table from TOM MCKINNEY.

TOM MCKINNEY
Anna Lee, thanks for meeting me for an ice cream. I know
your Dad and sister keep you busy. (Anna Lee is so shy that
he has to keep making conversation) You know, you're
different than your dad and your sister. (Awkwardly) Sorry.
What I meant is. Well, I don't know what I meant. Just
forget that.

So, your Pa said you moved here from Kentucky?

ANNA LEE shyly nods in the affirmative.

Cont. TOM MCKINNEY
(Long pause)I haven't had ice cream in a long time.
(Looking around)When I was a little kid my mom used to
always buy me an ice cream when we would come into

town. (Takes a bite of ice cream)Guess, growin' up in the
city you can have ice cream anytime you want.

(He looks intently at Anna Lee) Are you okay, Anna Lee?

ANNA LEE
(She looks up from the dish of ice cream, smiling broadly
and a bit naively) Thank you for asking me out. Can I tell
you something? It's kind of embarrassing, but I just want to
tell you.

TOM MCKINNEY
You can tell me anything Anna Lee.

ANNA LEE
Well, it's really stupid, but you are the first man who ever
asked me out. I mean, a lot of boys from school come
around, but my dad and Emily kind of scare them off. I
never had a man call for me, before. The reason I am telling
you is because I don't want you to think something is the
matter with me just because I am a little nervous.

TOM MCKINNEY (wide-eyed) He puts his hand out to her and holds it
tightly.

TOM MCKINNEY
Hey, Anna Lee. Relax, darlin'. If anybody ought to be
nervous it's me.

ANNA LEE
(Quietly)Really? Why?

TOM MCKINNEY
Well. I never in all my life ever met such a nice girl. And, I
can't hardly believe such a pretty girl would want to go out
with a dirty old cowboy like me. By the way, I was going to
shave, but something happened this morning and I couldn't
do everything I intended.

ANNA LEE
(Seriously) You know, you're very handsome.

TOM MCKINNEY

(With emphasis) Really? (Tom sits looking at her for a moment) Uh. By the way… The other reason I might be nervous is because when I went over to pick you up, I saw Emily. Emily explained that if I ever messed up and made you sad -or mad that she and ten truck drivers with tire irons would beat the crap out of me. (Seriously and trying to impress the significance) So, you see, Anna Lee, I really can't ever have you bein' all upset about anything.

                    ANNA LEE
                    (Laughing)
She wouldn't do that.

                    TOM MCKINNEY
(Seriously) Darlin' you just don't know how serious your sister was. I believe her. And, by the way, it wouldn't hurt if you put in a good word for me just to make sure there isn't ever any misunderstanding. Ten men with crow bars can mess a guy up for a long time.

INT. CHURCH WEDDING ALTAR. DAY.

Family and friends are gathered to see ANNA LEE AND TOM MCKINNEY get married.

                    COL. TOM MCKINNEY (V.O.)
Right at first, I sort of thought that I married Anna Lee because she was so pretty. Over the years, though, she became a part of me. She was my heart and soul. It's hard to explain. The first day I ever met Anna Lee, I knew she was the one. In later years a song came out that I knew was written for me and Anna Lee. I think it was called "Let it be me." Don't remember all the words, but it began, "I blessed the day I met you."

EXT. TOM MCKINNEY and ANNA LEE horseback riding.

Through a series of scenes (accelerated montage) we observe marital bliss of the young couple.

EXT. BARBEQUE. LARGE PARTY OF PEOPLE AT THE FRONT OF RANCH. DAY

INT. CHURCH. SUNDAY MORNING. DAY.

INT. BARN. LOFT. DAY.
The Couple rolling in the hay.

EXT. FRONT PORCH OF HOUSE. EVENING.
Couple in swing.

                    COL. TOM MCKINNEY (V.O.)
Life was good. Anna Lee was wonderful. I was happy. Pa
had graduated me out of riding herd with the boys.
Especially since trucking his cows straight from the ranch to
distant feed lots made him the first pile of money any of us
had ever seen.

Now, like I said before, none of us McKinney's or
Tumbleton's ever got too involved in goin' to war. I don't
know if any of my kin ever served in the Revolutionary War,
but if they did it's probably because they couldn't get out of
it. Running a big cattle ranch can get you exempted out of
military service, ordinarily. But, for some stupid reason
when World War II came around, I got it in my mind that it
would be a good idea to learn how to fly airplanes and go
kill Germans and Japanese.

INT. LARGE MAIN ROOM. EVENING.

In the great room we see ANNA LEE lightly sobbing, TOM MCKINNEY is
leaning against the fireplace, quietly. TOM'S best friend, COOP SAMSON
and his wife, SANDY are sitting together. JAKE is yelling.

                    JAKE
Are you crazy, boy. Why the hell would anybody want to go
half way around the world to get your ass blown off.

                    TOM MCKINNEY
I'm gonna be a pilot, Pa.

                    COOP SAMSON
Tom. You really do need to think this through.

                    TOM MCKINNEY
Coop. Come join with me. We can fly airplanes together.
It'll be great, man.

SANDY

Tom McKinney!! You leave Coop out of your hair-brained ideas. He has to finish law school. Every bit of trouble Coop ever got into, was your fault. You are not going to go draggin' him out of college to a war in Japan or Europe. That's something you would do!

Coop, we better go.

COOP SAMSON

Tom. Man you know I would go. But, we're gonna have kids and I almost have this law school thing knocked out. Don't go. Stay here and help Jake with the ranch. That's what you're supposed to do. This isn't wise.

JAKE

You cain't fly no damned aero plane. You can't even drive a car too good. You backed the tractor through the side of the barn. I ain't even sure you know how to turn on the radio. And, you think somebody is gonna teach you how to fly an aero plane. It ain't gonna happen and I don't wanna hear no more about it.

TOM MCKINNEY

Pa. I'm joining the air corps, tomorrow. They already told me they would take me and train me up at Randolph Field in San Antonio. I'm doin this. They said I was more mature than the others, too.

JAKE

That's just another way of saying that you are too old for this kind of foolishness. In another few years you'll be thirty. That's like a really old man in the Army.

INT. ANNA LEE and TOM'S BEDROOM. IN BED. NIGHT.

ANNA LEE

He's right, Tom. You're too old to go to war.

TOM MCKINNEY

No, I'm not. I'm just right. I know what I'm doin'. Can you imagine me flying one of those airplanes?

ANNA LEE

I don't want to, Tom.

                    TOM MCKINNEY
Don't worry, baby. This is the best way to go to war. All I
have to do is fly my airplane over Germany, drop bombs and
go home at night. That sounds easy; doesn't it?

                    ANNA LEE
So, you just fly over and drop bombs and go back to your
base?

                    TOM MCKINNEY
That's it. Easy as pie.

INT. COCKPIT B-24. INFLIGHT. EXPLOSION. DAY.

The pilot of the aircraft has just been brutally killed by an explosion on that
side of the plane. TOM MCKINNEY, (wearing Captain bars) is in the
copilot's seat. He has control of the airplane. There are explosions of flak
all around. A lot of noise.

                    TOM MCKINNEY
                    (Yelling at crew)
Pull him out of that seat and try to stop the
bleeding.

EXT. U.S. AIRFIELD IN LIBYA. DAY.

SUPERIMPOSE:

U.S. AIRFIELD - LIBYA - 1944

The B-24 is smoking, one prop is feathered. It flares and lands successfully.

INT. MESS HALL AT AIRFIELD. DAY.

Men are sitting at long tables eating. A full Colonel walks through the room
and stops at the table where TOM MCKINNEY is sitting. The Colonel has
something in his hand.

                    FULL COLONEL
(Grimly) Tom. Congratulations. You've been promoted to
Major. (He hands the oak leaf over) Good luck. (Walks
away)

INT. COCKPIT B-24. INFLIGHT. DAY.

This time, we see Major TOM MCKINNEY in the left seat of the airplane.
All seems peaceful.

                        COPILOT
        Well, that went well, Major. Looks like we're going to
        make it to happy hour without a scratch, tonight.

As he is speaking, a flight of two P-51 Mustangs pull along side.

                        TOM MCKINNEY
        We haven't made it yet. Man, I want to fly one of those
        Mustangs. I keep putting in for training and no one even
        responds.

                        COPILOT
        Well, Colonel, no offense but you may be too old for
        fighters. Hey, I can see the airfield.

                        TOM MCKINNEY
        Yeah. That's it. I guess seeing the airfield at the end of the
        day is a fairly good sign; isn't it?

INT. OFFICER'S CLUB at LIBYAN AIRFIELD. NIGHT.

Gentle and melancholy WWII music is heard playing over the other noises in
the club. There are men in flight suits at tables and at the bar. TOM
MCKINNEY is leaning against the bar talking to ANOTHER PILOT.
Again, the COLONEL is seen walking through the club.

                        TOM MCKINNEY
        Anyway, my plan is to get into training to fly P-51's. That
        has got to be the most beautiful airplane that has ever flown.
        They even named it after a horse: Mustang. It has a twelve
        cylinder Rolls Royce engine and swings four blades. It
        sounds like a fighter, looks like a fighter, and can stay
        overhead longer than anybody else's fighter. That is my
        airplane. I'm tellin' ya one of these days I am going to fly it.

                        OTHER PILOT AT THE BAR
        Uh-oh. Here comes the Colonel. He's probably handing out
        more field promotions. That's the last thing I want is to get

promoted in this man's army. Just puts you one step closer to getting somebody to replace you. Forever.

TOM MCKINNEY

I know what you mean. I think they pull the rank right off the dead body and hand it to his replacement.

The COLONEL walks up to TOM MCKINNEY.

TOM MCKINNEY

Why me, Colonel? Can't you find anybody else in this place stupid enough to promote?

COLONEL

Sorry, Tom. You're the oldest of all of us.

TOM MCKINNEY

So, we get promoted by our age?

COLONEL

Well, this is a big one. You're now the squadron commander. At least for a couple of months or so. (Hands TOM the silver oak leaf) Congratulations Colonel McKinney. (He walks away)

TOM MCKINNEY (To OTHER MAN AT BAR)

Well, I kind of like the sound of it, Colonel Tom McKinney.

INT. COCKPIT B-24. INFLIGHT. EXPLOSION. DAY.

COL. TOM MCKINNEY has been injured and is bleeding. He turns to the copilot (MIKE).

COL. TOM MCKINNEY

Mike. (Heavy, uneven breathing) You gotta decide whether to take this rig back across the Mediterranean or to ditch. I'm not gonna be with you much longer.

MIKE

Just hang on, Tom. (He readjusts a throttle, then over his shoulder he yells) Hey! You guys! Pull the Colonel out on the floor and make sure he isn't squirtin' blood.

We see two men pull COL TOM MCKINNEY from his seat and begin caring for him. There is still a lot of noise, shaking, gunfire, etc.

CREWMEMBER 1, leans up into the cockpit and speaks to MIKE.

CREWMEMBER 1
He isn't going to make it, Mike.

MIKE
Okay. How is everybody else?

CREWMEMBER 1
There are some cuts, burns, bumps, but I think we're okay. It's just the Colonel. I'm not a doctor, but he sure doesn't look too good. He might be able to make it back. Maybe not, I just don't know about stuff like that, Mike.

MIKE
I think this is the south coast of France maybe we could just ditch.

Suddenly there is a terrific EXPLOSION.

MIKE
Well, that settles that! Pop Tom's chute and push him out! Tell everybody to jump! (Screaming)Let's go, people! Everybody out, Now!

INT. FRANCE. COASTAL FARM. VERY SMALL ROOM WITH BED. NIGHT.

COL TOM MCKINNEY is lying in the bed asleep, but begins to open his eyes. Through very bleary eyes we see a young woman who is caring for him. His eyes close and the scene goes dark.

He opens his eyes again to see two women leaning over him, but he is too weak to comprehend and his eyes close as the scene goes dark once again.

INT. RANCH HOUSE MAIN ROOM. DAY.

(Meanwhile, back at the ranch) The DOCTOR is walking down the staircase. He gets to the bottom of the stairs where he is met by ANNA LEE. She appears concerned.

                    ANNA LEE
          Is Jake going to be alright, doctor?

                    DOCTOR
          Anna Lee, that bull trampled old Jake pretty bad. I
          recommend we move him to the hospital for a week or so.
          Would that be okay?

                    ANNA LEE
          Of course. Whatever you think. But he will be okay, right?

                    DOCTOR
          It's going to be awhile.

                    ANNA LEE
          I'll get some of the men to help get him to a car and to the
          hospital in the morning.

                    DOCTOR
          I'll check on him every day, Anna Lee. Uh, have you heard
          from Tom, lately.

                    ANNA LEE
          Oh, doctor. I am so worried. I haven't had a letter from him
          in almost two weeks. He has been so good to just send a
          note regularly. I have just been sick.

                    DOCTOR
          Well, I'm sure he's just fine. The boys are gonna wrap up
          that war real soon, I'm sure.

                    ANNA LEE
          I hope so. I wish he were here now.

INT. RANCH HOUSE MAIN ROOM. LATER THAT EVENING.

ANNA LEE hands one of the maids (ROSIE) (a young Mexican girl who
will age another forty years or so until the last few scenes) a stack of books.
There is a knock at the door.

                    ANNA LEE (To Rosie)
          That's okay, Rosie, I'll get it.

She opens the door. BENNETT (a trusted hand) is standing there with his hat in his hand.

                    ANNA LEE
Come in, Bennett.

                    BENNETT (entering)
Ms. Anna Lee I'm sorry to bother you with this again. But it's those three men Jake hired to take over for Billy.

                    ANNA LEE
Oh God, Bennett. Is there no end to this. First Billy dies, then Jake gets hurt. I wish Tom was here. Bennett I don't know what we should do about those men.(She looks up at him, hoping for help)

                    BENNETT
Well, ma'am. If I knew what to do, I would. But they've been stealing cows and now we think they have murdered one of the boys.

                    ANNA LEE
They killed somebody?!

                    BENNETT
It's that boy Sammy. He was found down by the east creek with a couple of bullets in his back. We think that down in that area, he saw something he wasn't supposed to. They shot him.

                    ANNA LEE
We need to call the sheriff.

                    BENNETT
(Looking quizzical)Ms. Anna Lee, no offense, but that ain't the way things like this ever get handled out here. The sheriff wouldn't even drive out here with what I'm here tellin' ya. We gotta take care of this. I'm thinkin' you just need to fire 'em off the place and me and a few of the boys will back you up with loaded guns. That'll be it.

                    ANNA LEE

Oh my. Am I supposed to go out there with a gun and fire a bunch of cattle rustlers? How in the world did it come to this. Oh, Bennett, I don't know if I can do this.

                    BENNETT
I don't know what else to tell you ma'am. What I mean is that it has got to be one of the owners of the ranch, who has the authority.

                    ANNA LEE
(Pause, thoughtfully) Well, I need to go to the hospital in the morning and see that Jake is all set up with everything he needs. Tomorrow night at the men's bunk house. Is it okay that I go out there?

                    BENNETT
Yes'm. About seven? I'll make sure we're ready.

INT. HOSPITAL HALLWAY. MORNING.

ANNA LEE is coming out of JAKE' room with a smile. As she turns, she sees EMILY (her sister) down the hall and calls out.

                    ANNA LEE
Emily! (Cheerfully) Is that you, Emily?

                    EMILY (With tears)
Anna Lee, what are you doing in town?

                    ANNA LEE
(With concern) I tried to call this morning, but no one would answer. What are you doing here?

EMILY looks into ANNA LEE'S eyes for a moment. ANNA LEE'S expression becomes fearful.

                    ANNA LEE
(Very quietly) Is daddy okay?

EMILY shakes her head negatively. ANNA LEE bursts into tears and falls into her sister's arms.

EXT. GRAVESIDE. DAY.

ANNA LEE and EMILY are standing near the open grave at the end of the service. People are leaving.

> EMILY
>
> Are you saying that you still haven't heard from Tom? What are you going to do? Are you going back out to the ranch?

> ANNA LEE
>
> Yes. I have to.

> EMILY
>
> Why? Why don't you just come stay with me here in town?

> ANNA LEE
>
> I have some very serious stuff that has been put off for too long, now. There was something I was supposed to do, but when daddy died, I just let it go. We've got rustlers and murderers running the place.

> EMILY
>
> Well, what do you intend to do about it, Anna Lee?

> ANNA LEE
>
> I'm going to go back to the ranch and shoot the sons of bitches.

> EMILY
>
> (Surprised) Anna Lee --?

> ANNA LEE
>
> Well, I'm afraid they're just catching me on a bad day.

INT. BUNK HOUSE. NIGHT.

Three very rough characters are facing ANNA LEE. Beside her is BENNETT and two other cowboys. The leader of the gang is SPIKE.

> SPIKE
>
> And I'm tellin' ya missy that I work for Jake McKinney. There ain't no sweet-assed little filly who can fire me off'n this place. Now, you go back up to the house and we won't have no more of this.

> ANNA LEE

(Forcefully)You and your thugs are fired. Get your stuff and get out, now.

Nervously, one of the men standing to SPIKE'S right pulls his gun and points it at her. ANNA LEE raises a gun that she has in her hand. Suddenly a gunshot is heard. Spike has a shocked look and pulls his gun and fires wildly. The man has shot ANNA LEE. Before she falls, she squeezes off a round that hits Spike's chest. Then, there is a flurry of gunfire by BENNETT and the other men, and the three thugs are all dead.

Men rush to ANNA LEE.

                    BENNETT
    Ms. Anna Lee! Hang on Anna Lee. Don't you die on me!

INT. FRANCE. VERY SMALL ROOM WITH BED IN FARM HOUSE. DAY.

This time, COL TOM MCKINNEY opens his eyes in a room that is lighted by the sun. He looks around the room trying to figure out where he is and how he got there. There are some sounds from the outer room. There is a sound of a woman's voice in French, speaking very loudly. Then, there is the sound of a man speaking German. Due to the sounds of anger, there is a small girl who is frightened and begins to cry. As COL MCKINNEY listens, he is dumfounded by what he is hearing. None of it makes sense. Suddenly, the door is kicked open by a very tall, well uniformed Nazi officer.

                    NAZI OFFICER
    Ah. What have we here? It is the American. (Arrogantly)
    My sweet Paulette, you have been seeing another man.
    Shame on you.

As the Nazi officer stares down at the very weak COL MCKINNEY, the Colonel looks back up at the Nazi with a most helpless expression. We see a full face view of the Nazi. He is arrogant and pompous. He unsnaps his gun holster. But, suddenly, before he can pull the gun, we hear an explosion of gunfire (one gunshot). The expression of the Nazi changes to one of shock as he crumples to the floor. One of the women has shot him in the back with a German pistol.

INT. VERY SMALL ROOM WITH BED IN FARM HOUSE. LATER THAT EVENING.

COL. MCKINNEY is sitting up in bed. There are two women who are sisters, PAULETTE and NICOLE. On the end of the bed is a four year old girl who is PAULETTE'S daughter, MARIE. The younger sister, NICOLE is feeding COL. MCKINNEY soup.

COL MCKINNEY
How did you happen to have that gun, Paulette?

PAULETTE
My sister, Nicole and I had to use a shovel to kill the last Nazi pig. We took his gun. It is not as easy to kill a hard headed Nazi with a shovel as you might think.

COL MCKINNEY
I suppose not. (He looks at the child)What's your name lady?

The child smiles broadly, but shyly hides her face.

NICOLE
This is Marie. She is Paulette's baby. I am aunt Nicole.

PAULETTE
She is aunt Nicole, but she pretends to be big sister, Nicole.

NICOLE (Smiling)
I always wanted a baby sister.

INT. ANNA LEE'S BEDROOM AT THE RANCH. NIGHT.

BENNETT
Anna Lee, the doctor has said you are going to be okay, but just need to get plenty of rest. The boy's are really braggin' about how you faced those killers down. Nobody has ever stood up for us like that before. (He drops his head)

ANNA LEE
There's something else, Bennett?

BENNETT
Yes ma'am. It's a telegram that I received for you.

ANNA LEE
(Closing her eyes) What, now? Read it, Bennett.

                    BENNETT
I did, Ms Anna Lee. It says Tom is missing. It says his plane
went down. They know that everybody bailed out over
southern France. They just haven't found all of them, yet.

Both remain silent for a very long time.

                    Cont. BENNETT
I heard on the radio today that the allied forces have stormed
the coast of France. The troops are in Paris. (After a long
pause) I don't even know where the hell Paris is. Guess I
ain't never been no place, except here.

                    ANNA LEE
Nobody ever needs to go to France. As soon as Tom comes
home from the war, I'm going to kill him.

                    BENNETT
Sounds like you're feelin' better.

                    ANNA LEE
Bennett, you're the new foreman of the Tumbleton. I need
you to take charge. I want you to do whatever you have to do
to make things work. I mean it.

                    BENNETT
Yes ma'am.

INT. FRANCE. FARM HOUSE. MAIN ROOM. DAY.

Inside the farm house, we see COL MCKINNEY sitting in a chair. He is
able to see the two sisters working in the garden outside the window. Inside,
the little girl MARIE is on the floor playing. Everything seems quiet and
peaceful.

Through the window, we see a Nazi vehicle drive up to the women and stop.
Two men get out. One of them takes a gun and shoots both women. COL
MCKINNEY is horrified at the sight.

COL MCKINNEY grabs MARIE and puts her in the small room and closes
the door.

EXT. FARM HOUSE. DAY.

102

The two Nazis begin walking toward the house. One is laughing. The other appears to be telling a story. When they get to the front door, one of the men turns the knob and pushes it open. As the door opens there is an explosion of gunfire and both Nazi's drop.

FADE TO BRIDGING SHOT

EXT. FRONT OF ORPHANAGE AT BORDEAUX FRANCE. DAY.

COL MCKINNEY is looking very well and is dressed in a clean uniform. There is a Jeep with a sergeant sitting at the wheel waiting for the Colonel. COL MCKINNEY is sitting on a bench leaning forward. MARIE is standing in front of him.

COL TOM MCKINNEY
Marie, you know I'm supposed to fly an airplane back to my home in San Antonio. (Pause) You understand, I must go home, don't you? (He looks around at the kids playing and fighting) You'll have lots of friends here.

(He looks away and sighs)Oh God, why does everything in this damned war have to be so hard.

Anyway, I saved a bunch of your stuff and put it in this bag. It has a picture of your mom and uh, well there wasn't a picture of your (pause)big sister, Nicole. (He sighs and tries to be serious) And, I got some papers here so everybody will know who you are. (He looks at the little girl for a long time) I'm going to give all this to the boss here. If I let you keep it, I'm afraid you will lose it or the other kids might, you know, steal it.

MARIE
(Softly) I'll be okay.

COL TOM MCKINNEY
(He stares at her for a long time. In a whisper) Oh God, please help me for what I am about to do.

EXT. AIRFIELD. IN FRONT OF A B-24. DAY.

There is a Jeep parked beside the aircraft and crewmembers are loading on board. All of the men get into the plane, except that COL TOM

MCKINNEY is finishing up with some of his personal gear. We see him begin to hand one last duffle bag through the door.

> COL TOM MCKINNEY
> (yells through the door from the outside)
> Mickey, this is the last one!

INT. B-24. DAY.

We see MICKEY lift the bag up and place it near the cockpit. COL MCKINNEY boards the aircraft and the door is slammed behind him. As he takes his seat we see MICKEY open the duffle bag. As the bag falls away, MARIE is standing there smiling.

> MICKEY
> (Smiles) Welcome aboard, Mademoiselle.

The engines are started and the aircraft begins to move.

> Cont. MICKEY
> And where would you like to go today ma'am.

> MARIE
> (With effort)San – An- tonio.

EXT. AIRFIELD RUNWAY. AIRPLANE TAKING OFF. DAY.

As the airplane breaks ground and the gear is coming up, the song "San Antonio Rose" is cued. This song continues through the next few scenes (accelerated montage) through the welcome home party.

EXT. AIRCRAFT FLYING OVER NORTH ATLANTIC. NIGHT.

EXT. AIRCRAFT FLYING OVER NEW YORK. DAY.

EXT. AIRCRAFT LANDING AT RANDOLPH AIRFIELD. SAN ANTONIO. DAY.

After the aircraft lands and the door is open, we see ANNA LEE, JAKE, BENNETT and a number of others waiting. COL MCKINNEY comes out of the plane after other crewmembers have exited. He has MARIE in his arms. ANNA LEE runs up and throws her arms around him and the child.

EXT. OUTSIDE THE RANCH HOUSE. WELCOME HOME BANNER, PARTY. NIGHT.

There is a stage with a band that will finish the song, "San Antonio Rose." As this tune continues we see hundreds of guests. There are lights and decorations and a large banner, "Welcome home Col. Tom." Everyone is dancing. JAKE has MARIE in his arms dancing, as she laughs vigorously for the first time.

As the camera finds ANNA LEE and COL TOM MCKINNEY, they are dancing closely and more slowly than all the rest.

INT. MASTER BEDROOM. RANCH. UPSTAIRS. NIGHT.

The room is somewhat dark. We can hear COL TOM MCKINNEY and ANNA LEE in bed. In the midst of very heavy breathing and physical exertion, ANNA LEE sits up in the bed and rises into camera view. She is damp and flushed and breathing hard. We see her smile broadly as COL TOM MCKINNEY sits up beside her.

ANNA LEE
(Catches her breath, then rhetorically and laughing) So, did ya miss me?

As COL TOM MCKINNEY rolls over on top of her we hear ANNA LEE let out a shrill screaming laughter that is heard down stairs.

INT. MAIN ROOM OF THE HOUSE. DOWNSTAIRS. NIGHT.

In the dimly lit room, we see ROSIE cleaning up litter that has been left from the party. She hears the shrill laughter from upstairs.

ROSIE
(Shaking her head) Aye, Yi, Yi.

INT. MASTER BEDROOM. DAY.

ANNA LEE is sitting in bed with MARIE. She holds the child closely and looks up at COL TOM MCKINNEY.

ANNA LEE
(Smiling) Tom, I think we might need a bunch more of these.

105

COL. TOM MCKINNEY (V.O.)

Anna Lee was right. We found that we were in grand need of some more little kids. First, was Jonathan. Then for awhile we thought we couldn't have any more kids and then along came my baby, Hanna.

INT. MAIN ROOM. RANCH. DAY.

JON is running around the room playing. The baby HANNA is in a walker and big sister, MARIE is feeding her.

COL. TOM MCKINNEY (V.O.)

Sometimes, when I would see Marie taking care of her little brother and sister, my mind would go back to my days in France. Somehow, it reminded me of Marie's young aunt, Nicole who always wanted to be a big sister. Marie was a natural. Over the years, Marie just naturally took over a lot of things. She was the big sister and she loved the role.

DISSOLVE TO BRIDGING SHOT

INT. DINING ROOM. TABLE SCENE. EVENING.

The family is around the table having dinner. The children are all practically adults. MARIE has brought her beau, JOSH.

Cont. COL. TOM MCKINNEY (V.O.)

Anna Lee and I were both surprised how we woke up one morning and all the kids were so grown up. The thing that really took the wind out of my sails was that evening when Marie brought Josh home for dinner. The boy had been coming around for years. Somehow, I just never gave any thought to the fact that they were up to getting married.

MARIE

Mom, Dad; we're getting married.

We see both, ANNA LEE and COL TOM MCKINNEY drop their jaws.

INT. HOSPITAL ROOM. DAY.

MARIE is in bed, holding a newborn baby.

COL. TOM MCKINNEY (V.O.)
Seems like the older you get the faster life seems to zip by.
It was like one moment, Anna Lee was having babies, then
all of a sudden, Marie was having babies. Sort of leaves a
man scratching his head and wondering where his life is
going. So, I did what any normal man would do. I went out
and bought me a new toy.

EXT. CRUDE DIRT AIRSTRIP. RANCH. DAY.

We see a beautiful new Beech-18 (airplane) landing on the airstrip.

EXT. RANCH AIRSTRIP. BESIDE BEECH-18. DAY.

COL. TOM MCKINNEY is excited, and happy to show his new airplane to
ANNA LEE. She appears ill at ease as she begins walking up the steps.

COL. TOM MCKINNEY
Honey, you're gonna love this thing. It's not as big as a B-
24, but it's a heck of a lot nicer.

INT. COCKPIT OF BEECH-18. DAY.

ANNA LEE is in the right seat. We see her white knuckles as she grips the
arm rests. COL TOM MCKINNEY is in the left seat and advances the
throttles.

COL TOM MCKINNEY
Here we go, Anna Lee. Watch how fast this thing gets off
the ground.

CRANE SHOT (AERIAL OVERHEAD)

As the tail wheel lifts off the ground we see the aircraft veer off the graded
airstrip and out across the country through the brush.

INT. COCKPIT OF BEECH-18. DAY.

COL TOM MCKINNEY looks serious and is working to control the aircraft.

ANNA LEE
(Screaming) then stops as the airplane becomes airborne.

Finally, the aircraft is airborne. All becomes quiet. We see a beautiful view as the aircraft flies across the ranch land.

> COL. TOM MCKINNEY (V.O.)
> It took me awhile at first to get the hang of flying a little airplane instead of a big old Army Air Corps bomber. Anna Lee never really cared that much for flying. Although, I think she did enjoy the flight. Flying wasn't enough for me though. Over the years I kept thinking that it would be fun to do some of the things I did when I was younger. So I spent a lot of time out with the boys doin' what we liked to do.

INT. STRIP CLUB. MEDIUM DARK. NIGHT.

COL TOM MCKINNEY is with some of his hired hands drinking and playing with the girls.

INT. DINING ROOM. LATE NIGHT.

JAKE is sitting at the dining room table. The table is clear (or clean). COL TOM MCKINNEY appears to be drunk and has a shotgun in his hands.

> JAKE
> Tom, you're just turnin' into a common drunk. All you do is drink, come home, and pass out. That ain't no life. You're already a grandpa and you got a boy who is about to start to college. Don't you think it's about time you grew up? And put that gun up before you shoot yourself!

> COL TOM MCKINNEY
> I was just tryin' to show you my new 12 gauge, and you have to start givin' me a ration. (Animated)Can't you ever just say, (falsetto)"Hey, that's nice." You always gotta get on my case about something. Anyway, I've been handling guns since I was a kid.

The gun goes off and flies out of his hand and knocks him to the floor. The dining room table is hit (but, we don't actually see the damage in this scene). ANNA LEE comes storming into the dining room from the bedroom. She picks up the gun.

> ANNA LEE

(Angry and impatiently, picks up the gun) Jake, put this up. (Handing the shotgun)

(To COL MCKINNEY) To bed, now! Tom. (She points to the other end of the house) Are both of you out of your minds? It must be two in the morning. Now, go to bed, Tom.

Jake, make sure that thing's not loaded before you put it up. (Both men silently do as they are told)

INT. DINING ROOM. MORNING BREAKFAST.

As the family is sitting around the table for breakfast, ROSIE comes through and announces BENNETT (foreman) has arrived.

JAKE

Bennett! Come in. Have some breakfast.

BENNETT

Just coffee, Sir.

As Bennett sits down at the table, (for the first time) we see a large gaping hole in the table that was made with the shotgun the night before. Bennett looks but chooses not to say anything.

EXT. BULL PENS. DAY.

JAKE is seen in one of the pens. Over his shoulder, we see a large bull charging him from behind.

EXT. GRAVESIDE. DAY.

Large group of mourners are at the funeral for Jake.

COL. TOM MCKINNEY (V.O.)

We had a bad year. Our housekeeper, Rosie, was attacked and hurt real bad by a couple of no-good, no-account thugs. I think she got over it, but then, the prosecutor dropped the ball and the men got released. On the way out of the courthouse door, they looked right at Rosie and Anna Lee and then had the gall to threaten Anna Lee. Then, right after that, Jake was killed by one of his bulls. (Pause) We all went to Disney Land. Anna Lee thought it was an awful thing to do. I had to practically tie her up and put her on the plane.

INT. BEECH-18. CABIN. DAY.

Inside the cabin, are ANNA LEE, JON, HANNA and EMILY. HANNA is sitting across from EMILY. HANNA is 12-13 years old. She is looking at her aunt EMILY suspiciously. Finally, she leans forward and speaks to EMILY. (COL TOM MCKINNEY is in the cockpit.)

                    HANNA
          Aunt Emily. (Pause) I know why we're going to Disney
          Land.

EMILY looks at the young girl for a moment. Then, very seriously, she holds one finger up to her lips indicating that she should keep her knowledge to herself. Emily gently moves her head from side to side indicating, "no."

EXT. DISNEY LAND. DAY.

All are wandering through the amusement park.

                    COL. TOM MCKINNEY (V.O.)
          To top everything off, Anna Lee's sister, Emily, had a heart
          attack and died in Anaheim, California. We probably just
          spent too hard a day chasing the kids around to all the rides.
          Anna Lee was very upset.

EXT. GRAVESIDE. DAY.

Large number of people are gathered at the funeral.

                    COL. TOM MCKINNEY (V.O.)
          For awhile, it seemed that all we ever did was go to funerals.
          I guess it is in bad taste to mention, but as it turned out,
          Anna Lee became the sole heir to the Bower's Trucking
          company. After all those years, it turned out that I ended up
          marryin' a rich girl. It got left up to me to manage the
          operation, but I didn't really mind.

EXT. BOWERS TRUCKING CO. DAY.

Large fleet of trucks in action.

110

COL TOM MCKINNEY (V.O.)
Fact is. Well, it was during that same time frame that we
started drilling for oil and gas. Got our own drilling
company. Then we found out that the city slickers would pay
a fortune for hunting leases. We also found out that those
buckin' bulls that Pa spent so much time breeding were
really valuable. We got into breeding expensive horses
while we were at it. The ranch was really turning into a
major industry for the first time in over a century. I'll have to
admit, though, it was the Bowers Trucking company that old
Emily took care of for so long that was really valuable. She
had railroad permits that were worth a fortune. She had
deals cut with the unions that nobody else could compete
with. Emily had turned that trucking company into the
biggest in the state.

I bought me a turboprop airplane.

INT. REYNOSA, MEXICO. STRIP CLUB. NIGHT.

COL TOM MCKINNEY is with a group of men, drinking and playing with
the girls.

COL. TOM MCKINNEY (V.O.)
My theory was that if you work real hard, you ought to play
really hard, too. It was four or five years later. A bad thing
happened. I guess over all those years, I must have known it
was coming. Anyway, one night, me and the boys were
down in Reynosa a little too late. I forgot that I had an
important meeting at the ranch the next morning. That is I
forgot, until I remembered at four in the morning. I called
one of the pilots to fly down and get me. They picked me up
at McAllen airport about six that morning.

EXT. RANCH AIRSTRIP. IMPROVED AND PAVED. EARLY
MORNING.

We realize the sun is just coming up (roosters crowing, music etc.) We see
his new corporate sized turbo-prop landing at the ranch.

INT. MASTER BEDROOM. RANCH. MORNING.

As COL TOM MCKINNEY enters the bedroom, he looks disheveled.
ANNA LEE is dressed, the bed is made and all is in order. He looks very

much out of place. ANNA LEE only looks at him as he comes through the room. COL TOM MCKINNEY heads straight for the bathroom. We hear him retching over the toilet. We hear him washing. ANNA LEE is still in the bedroom, seething. He comes out of the bathroom and heads for the door.

COL TOM MCKINNEY
I've got a meeting with Mack Truck down stairs, right now.
You look pissed off, so I'll just talk to ya later, darlin'.

INT. STUDY. DAY.

It appears that the meeting is completed; all of the men stand up, shake hands and begin moving to the door.

INT. FRONT FOYER. DAY.

ANNA LEE and HANNA (now 18-19) are dressed and walking out the front door. HANNA is teary eyed. A pile of suit cases are being carried out of the house by one of the hired hands (DICK) whose demeanor implies that he is a dimwit. As ANNA LEE and HANNA are about to get into the car, they are stopped by COL TOM MCKINNEY.

COL TOM MCKINNEY
Where the hell are you goin' Anna Lee?

ANNA LEE
Hanna and I are going to move to San Antonio for awhile.

COL TOM MCKINNEY
What does that mean?

ANNA LEE
It means that I have had all of you I can stand for awhile.
You're a drunk. What's worse is (pause) other women!

COL TOM MCKINNEY
What are you talking about; other women! You can't leave.
I won't let you, Anna Lee.

ANNA LEE
You try to stop me, Tom McKinney and you'll be sorry.

EXT. FRONT PORCH. DAY.

112

The entire group begins moving to the front porch as the car is loaded.

COL TOM MCKINNEY
What do you mean I'll be sorry. What are you gonna do?

ANNA LEE
I could shoot you and drop you right here in the dirt and
there's not a man on this place who would blame me.

DICK (The "slow" hired hand) walks adjacent to Anna Lee as he is loading
her bags.

DICK (To COL MCKINNEY)
(Deadpan, serious and nodding)
It's true, Boss.

ANNA LEE gets into the backseat of the car. HANNA hugs her father.

HANNA
Daddy, I have to go with mom. If I don't she'll be all by
herself.

COL TOM MCKINNEY
Baby, you call me every night. And. And. And, tell your
mom that I have decided to join that alcoholic "AA" thing in
San Antonio that she talks about.

HANNA
Okay.

COL TOM MCKINNEY
And, also, Hanna. Hanna. Maybe I'll give it a few days and
when I come up to San Antonio for the AA, you and your
mom and me we'll have dinner. Tell her that, okay.

HANNA
I will.

OFFSCREEN ANNA LEE
Hanna! Come get in the car.

The car drives off. COL TOM MCKINNEY sits down on the porch.
BENNETT walks up to him.

BENNETT

You must have really stepped in it this time, colonel.

COL TOM MCKINNEY

Bennett, what did she mean when she said nobody would
blame her for shootin' me?

BENNETT

Boss, you know that legend the boys have about her.

COL TOM MCKINNEY

You mean shootin' all the cattle rustlers. I think the number
is up to a half dozen now, isn't it?

BENNETT

Or, maybe more. They think she's a saint. She could lead
every man on this place into the fires of hell. It's just that
people build things up over the years. They like Anna Lee.
She's done some good stuff for the boys, the maids, the
Mexicans and some of the families. They like her.

COL TOM MCKINNEY

So, what do they think of me, Bennett?

BENNETT

(Hesitantly) Oh. Well. They pretty much just think you're uh
asshole, boss.

EXT. SAN ANTONIO RIVERWALK. DAY.

HANNA and COL MCKINNEY are sitting on a bench watching the
HILTON PALACIOS HOTEL being constructed (Historic construction).

COL TOM MCKINNEY

So, when does the World's Fair begin, Hanna?

HANNA

It starts next week, Daddy. In fact, mom got notice that the
daily rate on our hotel was going to go up to over fifty
dollars a day.

COL TOM MCKINNEY

Do you think your mom is about ready to come home, baby?

114

HANNA
God, I hope so. I am so tired of staying in that place.

The two sit and watch the construction for awhile.

Cont. HANNA
Daddy. Can I tell you a story.

COL TOM MCKINNEY
What?

HANNA
Daddy, I just wanted to tell you that some things just stink
worse than other things. Do you remember my boyfriend, in
high school; Jeff?

COL TOM MCKINNEY
Yeah, I remember him. He was a good kid. He was the
receiver who made two touchdowns in the championship
game during your senior year. Whatever happened to him? I
thought he was a nice boy.

HANNA
He was. He was alright, I guess. Anyway, that night after
we won that game, Linda and I went back to the locker
rooms. I mean, you know, out in the main hall. So, when
the guys were heading for the showers we were going to
meet them. Jeff and Linda and Steve and I were going to a
party that night. So, we were all excited and jumping up and
down and all that. Then, the guys came into the building and
I was going to give him a hug or something. Well, Jeff had
pulled his shirt off and when he got to me, he just pushed my
face into his arm pit.

COL TOM MCKINNEY
I don't get it. Why did he do that?

HANNA
Because he was just a stupid high school kid running on a
double dose of adrenaline, I guess. So, what happened was
that I decided to kill him. But, when he came back out of the
locker room, he saw how mad I was. I started hitting him
and then immediately realized that beating up a
championship football player might be futile. Well, he

dropped to his knees, begged for forgiveness and then we all went to the party and danced all night. And, that's the end of that story.

COL TOM MCKINNEY
I still don't get it, baby.

HANNA
Well, after we started to college, Linda and Steve decided to get married. Jeff went to Steve's bachelor party. I knew they were going to drink and I knew they were going to have naked girls and all that stupid stuff that guys do. Well, later that night, Jeff came by. He was a little drunk, but nothing too serious. When he came in, Daddy, he smelled. Do you know what he smelled like?

COL TOM MCKINNEY
Well, I can imagine.

HANNA
Dad, those girls put on body make up. They wear a lot of perfume. Then they work out equal to a couple of hours of aerobics. Then, they rub up against the guys and they leave make up, perfume and body odor. That smell, Daddy, is the most identifiable smell there is. The smell of a girl that has been rubbing up against your boyfriend or husband is the most vile smell in the universe. Having your face pushed into a football players armpit is nothing compared to that smell. It hurts. It hurts in a place you can't rub. There is not a pill you can take for it. It just hurts. I'm sorry, Daddy, but I think you have done that to mom more than once. You need to be nice to her. And, you need to stop behaving like a college boy at a bachelor party. ...I'm sorry. And, I love you.

COL TOM MCKINNEY puts his arm around HANNA.

COL TOM MCKINNEY (Quietly)
Oh, my little baby, Hanna. When did you grow up to be so smart?

INT. HOTEL ROOM. AFTERNOON.

116

HANNA is lying on a bed facing the camera, looking at a magazine. ANNA LEE is walking back and forth through the room in b.g., busy gathering stuff to be packed in the open suit cases.

HANNA

Dad said that he would pick us up about six. Boy, will I be glad to go home and get out of this shit-hole.

Immediately, she clinches her teeth and cringes as she makes the statement.

ANNA LEE

HANNA!!!! (Screaming) How many times do I have to tell you! That's it lady! You are going to a convent!

She grabs HANNA by the arm and drags her off the bed.

HANNA

Right now?!

ANNA LEE

Right now, I am going to wash your mouth out, just the way I always promised! Then you're going to a convent, forever!

HANNA

MOM!!! You don't even know what a convent is, mom! I don't think we're even Catholic!

INT. BATHROOM.

The two have struggled into the bathroom and on their knees by the tub.

ANNA LEE

I'll tell you what a convent is young lady!! It's a place with really mean nuns and there are no boys and you have to wear a long black uniform.

ANNA LEE is struggling with HANNA over the side of the bath tub.

HANNA

Gees, mom, I'm sorry! Stop it! MOTHER!!!

ANNA LEE picks a bar of soap out of the bath/shower soap dish and forces it into HANNA'S mouth. As soon as the bar is in Hanna's mouth she let's go and stands up.

117

HANNA spits the bar out.

HANNA
(Screaming) MOTHER ARE YOU CRAZY!!!!

HANNA goes to the sink and continues to spit and rinse her mouth.

HANNA
God almighty, mother. I just got through washing my butt with that bar of soap!

ANNA LEE
You wanna do it again?

HANNA
No ma'am. ......Mother, you are certifiable. I'm going to tell daddy what you did. You can send me to a convent or or whatever you want, but me and daddy are going to send you to the crazy house. Gees.

ANNA LEE
Truer words have never been spoken, sweetheart. You and your father will be my ticket straight to an insane asylum.

INT. HOTEL BEDROOM.

HANNA jumps back on the bed and pulls out the magazine, again.

HANNA
I guess I should be more careful around you, mother. I mean after all, I hear that you killed ten men for stealing cows.

ANNA LEE
What are you talking about?

HANNA
That's what all the guys out on the ranch say. Once you killed ten cattle rustlers while dad was in the War.

ANNA LEE
(Hesitantly) I did no such thing.

HANNA

Well, something happened. I know you still have a bullet scar in your side.

ANNA LEE

Hanna, that didn't happen. Have you ever heard Bennett say such a thing?

HANNA

He was there when I heard it.

ANNA LEE

What did he say?

HANNA

He just told everybody to get back to work; then he walked away. I know lots of stuff, mom.

ANNA LEE

Like what?

HANNA

I know why we took that trip to Disney Land, after grandpa died. Do you?

We see ANNA LEE idly folding clothes for the suitcase.

ANNA LEE

No. I never knew why we went there. That was the worst trip in my life. Poor Emily. I think that she just wasn't up for hiking around that place. She didn't want to go. I don't know why she was so insistent about going.

HANNA

I know why, mom. You want me to tell you.

ANNA LEE

(Bored)Why did we go Hanna?

HANNA

Are you sure you want me to tell you?

ANNA LEE

Are you sure you don't want me to hold your head down in the toilet for awhile?

HANNA

Well, ok. Before we left I heard daddy talking to aunt Emily
about those bad guys who attacked Rosie. He told Emily he
was going to kill them because he thought they were going
to hurt you.

In the background, we see ANNA LEE place the clothes down and look
more seriously at HANNA.

ANNA LEE

(Quietly) But that didn't happen?

HANNA

No. But the reason it didn't happen is that aunt Emily told
daddy that he could get the death sentence in Texas for
killing them. So, she said that she would get some of her
truck drivers and beat the shit out of them. Mom! Her words,
not mine.

ANNA LEE

(Quietly) But, that didn't happen either?

HANNA

(Laughingly)Huh! That's the reason Daddy and Emily
ended up in the same plane on the same day headed for
Disney Land of all places on earth. They were like, --out of
town when it happened.

ANNA LEE

But, it didn't happen.

HANNA

Remember that night when we got back to the ranch? You
were trying to tell daddy something and he was watching the
news? And, you couldn't get him to pay attention to you?
And, you got mad because he wouldn't listen to you? I think
you were talking about Emily's funeral.

ANNA LEE

(Seriously) I do remember.

HANNA

Well, if you had been watching the news you would have seen that those men were beat half to death. The news said that they would be in the hospital and then in physical therapy for a year or so.

ANNA LEE

Hanna. Have you ever told anyone else about this?

HANNA

No.

ANNA LEE

Baby. You can never speak of this again. Your father could get in a lot of trouble if anyone ever put all that together.

HANNA

I won't ever say anything.

ANNA LEE

You can never tell your sweetest, sweetheart, or your best girl friend or anybody, ever. It would be better if you didn't tell Marie or Jon. Honey, do you understand how bad it could be, if anyone ever found out?

HANNA

I'm not going to tell anybody.

ANNA LEE

Maybe you should not even tell your father that you know about that. Have you ever told him, or anyone?

HANNA

(Frightened)I said, "no."

EXT. TUMBLETON AIRSTRIP. DAY. LATE AFTERNOON.

We see COL. MCKINNEY and ANNA LEE parked on the ramp of the Tumbleton airfield. The Col. is leaning up against the car near the passenger window. Anna Lee is inside the car with the window rolled down.

COL. MCKINNEY

He's a civil engineer. He's a good guy. As a kind of sponsor, he is supposed to give me moral support when I get a hankerin' to get drunk. If you ask me, ol' Miller and me woulda' been a couple of good drinkin' buddies if it weren't for the fact that we are in the AA together.

COL. MCKINNEY smiles at the idea.

> ANNA LEE
> So, Tom, what happened when you went over to apologize to Neal?

> COL TOM MCKINNEY
> Anna Lee, I swear, girl. You know, this AA thing is going to finally be the death of me babe. I went over there nice as I can be. That ole sumbitch actually tried to kill me, honey. If his old lady hadn't turned the garden hose on us, I probably woulda hurt that old fart.

> ANNA LEE
> Well, what did you say to him? Didn't you apologize?

> COL TOM MCKINNEY
> Well, yeah.

> ANNA LEE
> What do you mean, "Well, yeah?" What does that mean?

> COL TOM MCKINNEY
> Well, it's kinda complicated, darlin'. I think the plane will be here pretty quick; do you see it, or hear it?

> ANNA LEE
> Tom. Tell me what happened.

> COL TOM MCKINNEY
> Honey, it's like this. I thought he was all pissy-faced because our drilling company undercut him. I mean, Anna Lee, we made about ten million on that deal before it was all said and done. But, as it turned out, he didn't even know it was us who undercut him.

> ANNA LEE
> So, that's why he beat you up?

> COL TOM MCKINNEY

122

Dammit, Anna Lee. How many times do I have to tell you,
woman. He didn't beat me up. Why do you keep saying that?

ANNA LEE
Anyway, that's what the fight was about?

COL TOM MCKINNEY
Well, not exactly. Turns out, he was all mad, because he
thought I ran over his stupid dog a couple of years ago when
all us guys were hunting down south.

ANNA LEE
You ran over his dog?

COL TOM MCKINNEY
(Weakly) Maybe.

ANNA LEE
Did you apologize for that.

COL TOM MCKINNEY
APOLOGIZE!? I ain't gonna apologize for runnin' over the
stupidest dog that ever went on a huntin' trip. Anyway, it
wasn't my fault. That stupid dog kept runnin' in front of my
pickup.

ANNA LEE
(Softly) Oh, Tom. I'm afraid if you keep going around
apologizing for all the stupid drunk things you've done, one
of your dear, best friends is going to kill you.

COL TOM MCKINNEY
Exactly. Now, you see what I'm sayin', Anna Lee.

ANNA LEE
Maybe it would be better if you would just run a full page ad
in the San Antonio Express and apologize to the world in
general for being such a jackass.

COL TOM MCKINNEY
And, there she is. My loving and supportive wife. Thank you
--Anna Lee.

ANNA LEE

Tom, I see your plane.

                    COL. MCKINNEY
Yeah, that's them. (Thoughtfully) Baby, I'm thinkin' about
buyin' us a jet. What do you think?

                    ANNA LEE
That's just what we need, another airplane, Tom.

              COL MCKINNEY (absent mindedly)
Yeah, that's what I was thinkin'.

We see ANNA LEE roll her eyes.

COL MCKINNEY'S turbo-prop lands and taxis up near the car. As the
engines are shut down and we hear the turbines wind down, ANNA LEE gets
out of the car and stands near COL. MCKINNEY.

The air stair door opens on the airplane and at first we see a PILOT #1, who
then stands aside as MILLER comes to the door. MILLER begins to walk
down the steps, but stumbles, grabs a hand (rail, chain, cable). As he
continues to fall PILOT #1 lunges out the door to aid MILLER.

COL. MCKINNEY and ANNA LEE stand by the car helplessly.

MILLER is at the foot of the steps lying quietly with the PILOT #1 leaning
over him. The PILOT #1 looks up at COL. MCKINNEY.

                    PILOT #1
Boss, we tried to stop him. (Pause) He got into the bar and
choked down a lot of booze. Boss, he's dead drunk.

PILOT #2 comes down the steps of the plane.

                    PILOT #2
COL., he really soaked up a lot of liquor. I mean he absorbed
it faster than we could do anything about it. (long pause)
Sorry, COL.

What do you think we should do? Do you want to take him
up to the house.

              ANNA LEE (to COL. MCKINNEY)
We should take him up to the house. He looks really bad.

124

COL. MCKINNEY considers the situation.

> COL. MCKINNEY
> No. (He looks around) Take him back to San Antonio.

> ANNA LEE
> But, Tom. Don't you think we should take care, to see that he gets sobered up?

> COL. MCKINNEY
> Naw. I don't think so.

> ANNA LEE
> But, we should do something, Tom.

> COL. MCKINNEY (to the PILOTS)
> Load him back on the plane, boys. Take him back to San Antonio.

> PILOT #2
> What do we do with him when we get him back to San Antonio, Col.?

> COL. MCKINNEY (Thoughtfully)
> Why don't you find him a quiet, safe place to sober up and wake up.

The PILOTS begin carrying MILLER back up the steps of the plane. As the aircraft lifts off, we again see ANNA LEE with concern on her face as she speaks to COL. MCKINNEY.

> ANNA LEE
> Tom, aren't you suppose to sort of take care of MILLER when he gets like that? Shouldn't you have done something?

> COL. MCKINNEY
> See darlin' that's the difference between you and me. You ask, "shouldn't you have done somethin'?" And me, I'm thinkin' I just sent a drunk home on a multi-million dollar corporate turboprop.

After a thoughtful moment…

Cont. COL. MCKINNEY
I suppose, if I could have done anything, I could have
restocked the liquor locker, for him.

ANNA LEE
Well, I just hope he's okay.

COL. MCKINNEY
He'll be alright. Drunks just want to be left alone when they
finally drop. At least he doesn't have to face you and me in
the morning. He'll be home in San Antonio.

EXT.– SAN ANTONIO AIRPORT – RAMP AT (RAYTHEON FBO).
NIGHT.

The Tumbleton airplane taxis onto the ramp and shuts down it's engines. As
the doors open the two PILOTS are helping MILLER down the steps.
MILLER is walking, but is still definitely "out of it."

INT.– RAYTHEON OFFICE LOBBY FOR PASSENGERS. NIGHT.

As the PILOTS walk MILLER into the empty lobby, an ATTRACTIVE
YOUNG WOMAN #1 at the counter looks at the PILOTS and MILLER.

ATTRACTIVE YOUNG WOMAN #1
May I help you?

PILOT #2
We've got a passenger who may need to catch an hour's
snooze.

ATTRACTIVE YOUNG WOMAN #1
Maybe the pilots' lounge?

PILOT #1
Yeah, that'd be good.

PILOT #2
Let's go.

As they are walking MILLER down the hallway, PILOT #1 sees the inside of
a large, empty, conference room.

PILOT #1

Hey, this will be better. There won't be anybody in here all night.

PILOT #2

Yeah, that's good.

We watch the two PILOTS wrestle MILLER into one of the chairs about midway down one side of a giant, luxurious conference table. MILLER lays his head on the table with his hands palm down and close to his head. The PILOTS hang his suit coat on the back of the chair. One of the PILOTS looks at the scene and grabs some paper from a side table and stuffs them under MILLER'S hands. The other pilot picks up a pencil and sticks it between MILLERS fingers as though he had been writing something, before he fell asleep.

PILOTS
(to each other and in reaction to the scene)
Slight snicker

EXT.– SAN ANTONIO AIRPORT- RAYTHEON RAMP. MORNING.

A large corporate jet taxis onto the ramp and shut down. When the door is opened there are approximately six well dressed BUSINESS MEN AND WOMEN who walk down the steps and toward the Raytheon office.

INT. INSIDE RAYTHEON OFFICE LOBBY. MORNING.

As the BUSINESS MEN AND WOMEN enter the lobby they are greeted by another group of similarly dressed BUSINESS MEN AND WOMEN.

BUSINESS WOMAN #1
We have a conference room reserved down the hall.

She turns to the ATTRACTIVE YOUNG WOMAN #2 behind the counter.

Cont. BUSINESS WOMAN #1
Is the conference room ready for us?

ATTRACTIVE YOUNG WOMAN #2
Yes. (Tentatively) I think that some of your party may have arrived early. It looked like someone was in there waiting for you.

INT. CONFERENCE ROOM. DAY.

MILLER is still sitting in the chair where he was left the night before. Everyone else files in and either sits down, gets coffee, or starts setting up their (PowerPoint) briefing.

After awhile, everyone is seated and it appears that they are about to begin. A MAN at the front of the room appears to be ready to begin his briefing.

Among several camera shots, we see a briefing where a couple of different people (MAN #2 AND #3) stand at the front of the room. Then, MAN #1 goes to the front of the room.

                    MAN #1
The man looks unapprovingly of MILLER who is still sleeping soundly. He makes a gesture at a man sitting next to MILLER indicating that he should be awakened. Then he continues his briefing.

                    Cont. MAN #1
        …… So, the plan right now is that we will have seven
        pumping stations up the side of this geographic rise…

As the briefing continues, we see MILLER awakened. He sits straight up. His tie is turned slightly crooked. We can see the thoughts going through his mind. He calmly looks around the room for a familiar face. After only a moment he gently turns his head and looks around the room to see a familiar sight within the room. He has no idea where he is. He turns toward the briefer and shows a sincere interest in the topic.

Then, in an instant, MILLER reaches for his tie and straitens it, followed by running his fingers through his thin hair. He turns again to the briefer, MAN #1, and as we see MILLER now, he looks most dignified and very much a part of the meeting.

                    Cont. MAN #1
        Right now, we have estimated the costs to run close to one
        billion, but that price will be reassessed after we get onsite in
        South Africa.

        The primary issue is running this water uphill over a distance
        of two hundred miles and up an elevation rise of four
        hundred seventy feet. We will try to get another engineering
        company to look at other options that could help.

Let me show you the plan on the pumping stations.

MAN #1 puts up another slide.

                    MILLER
(Hoarsely) Pardon me?

                    MAN #1
Yes? Do you have a question?

                    MILLER
(A little choked up) Are you developing, (he coughs) from
scratch seven manned pumping stations with reservoirs?

                    MAN #1
Yes. (Pause) Sir, (snidely) you may have been asleep during
that part of the briefing. May I ask, Sir, who you are? Are
you with Benning Petroleum? I don't think I have met you.

                    MILLER
No. In fact, I don't know for sure who invited me to your
meeting. But, I can sure tell you why they invited me.

                    MAN #1
So, you're not with our company? Sir, this is a private
meeting.

                    MILLER
Well, let me explain. I think that one of your people invited
me here for a reason.

                    MAN #1
What? I mean, what reason?

                    MILLER
Well, as it turns out, I am very familiar with the issues you
have been talking about. In fact, my company has had a lot
of first hand experience with making water run uphill. My
associates and I have worked the Suez Canal, the Panama
Canal and the latest flood controls from one end of the
Mississippi to New Orleans. If I may? (he indicates that he
would like to go to the board at the front of the room).

                    MAN #1

Okay. (weakly)

MILLER

Let me show you something.(begins drawing on the board)

I think you can eliminate the reservoirs, and the high performance pumps if you do something we did on the aqueduct outside L.A. Now, what it requires is a bit more pipe. But in the end, if you have any pesky environmentalists, this will really shut 'em up when you show them your alternative.

What we want to do…

COL TOM MCKINNEY (V.O.)

After that fiasco, I didn't make it back to the AA meetings the way I should. It was a good place. Met some of the smartest and most interesting people I ever knew. I heard from Miller. He called me one night from Cape Town, South Africa braggin' about the fact that he had just made a million dollars. Years later I heard that he fell off an eighth floor hotel balcony. He was one of those fallin' down kind of drunks. I always liked old Miller. I probably shoulda been a better friend.

BRIDGING SHOT.

INT. RANCH. MAIN ROOM AND WALK THROUGH DINING ROOM. DAY.

As ANNA LEE walks through the two rooms we see a number of workers with saw-horses, drop cloth, etc. The house is being renovated or remodeled. ANNA LEE is a bit bewildered. First, she sees HANNA then, HANNA sees JON.

ANNA LEE (To HANNA)

Hanna you haven't changed yet.

HANNA

It's just Marie and Josh and the babies.

JON (To HANNA)

What's going on tonight, anyway?

HANNA

It's family night (rolling her eyes).

JON

That's never good. Somebody usually tries to kill somebody
else at mother's family night thing.

HANNA

Tell me about it.

INT. DINING ROOM. DINING ROOM TABLE IS SET EXQUISITELY.
EVENING.

Around the table are COL TOM MCKINNEY, ANNA LEE, MARIE, JOSH,
HANNA, JON, AND TWO VERY YOUNG CHILDREN. MARIE is
feeding the youngest. HANNA is sitting next to MARIE. JON is sitting
across from HANNA.

HANNA

So, do you want me to tell you what I saw Jon doing with
Susan?

MARIE puts her arm around HANNA and then gently puts her hand over
HANNA'S mouth.

MARIE

We don't need to stir anything up, baby.

JON

Yeah. In fact, maybe we could talk about where you were
Saturday night.

MARIE holds up one finger to JON indicating that he stop saying whatever
he is about to say. As soon as she makes that signal JON closes his mouth
and leans back in his chair.

MARIE

So, daddy. Josh and I are thinking that in five years or so,
when the kids are a little older, we are going to go to France.

JOSH

Maybe even five or ten years from now.

MARIE

Yes baby. Whatever you say. Anyway, I was thinking that you and mother could go with us.

COL TOM MCKINNEY
I have no interest in going back to France. I once landed there in a parachute and decided that I would never go back.

MARIE
But, daddy, what about mom. She wants to go. Don't you mother?

ANNA LEE
Oh sweetheart. I really would like to go. That far in the future, we might. I have this house all torn to pieces and I am beginning to wonder if I will ever get it put back.

COL TOM MCKINNEY
This house is the biggest mess I…

MARIE
(Emphatically) Daddy.

COL TOM MCKINNEY
Well, I'm just saying…

MARIE
Well, don't. It is going to be beautiful when mom gets finished and you're going to love it. This place has needed remodeling since the first world war.

INT. THE MASTER BEDROOM. LIGHTS OUT AND DIM LIGHTING. NIGHT.

COL. MCKINNEY and ANNA LEE are both lying in bed on their backs, seemingly staring at the ceiling.

ANNA LEE
Tom, I know you don't like to talk about this, but you know how I kind of let you off the hook for your AA apology program?

COL TOM MCKINNEY
Oh, Anna Lee, do we have to start that again?

ANNA LEE

It's just Coop Samson.

COL TOM MCKINNEY

Old Coop.

ANNA LEE

He is your best friend in the whole world, Tom. You need to
take care of that problem. I really want you to. He is the
nicest friend. He is the most honorable man you ever got
drunk with. And, you and he have been friends ever since
high school.

COL TOM MCKINNEY

He sued me, Anna Lee. The San Antonio district attorney
sued my ass for four thousand dollars, Honey.

ANNA LEE

So your friendship with Coop is not worth four thousand
dollars?

COL TOM MCKINNEY

You know it's not the money, Anna Lee. How dare he sue
me. I'm his best friend. He's the D.A. He sues me because
he thinks he can slap me around in the court house.

ANNA LEE

Well, you showed him, didn't you?

COL TOM MCKINNEY

Nobody is gonna push me around. If he had asked real nice-
like, I woulda given him any amount of money he wanted.

ANNA LEE

That's when you paid off a federal judge to have it thrown
out.

COL TOM MCKINNEY

I never did any such thing. And, furthermore, I would
appreciate if my own wife wouldn't go around accusing me
of such things. Do you know how serious that is? Stop
sayin' that. Anyway, he actually complained that I
threatened Judge Perry. Which I didn't.

ANNA LEE

Regardless of all else, Tom. I want you to promise me one thing.

COL TOM MCKINNEY

What?

ANNA LEE

I want you to apologize to Coop.

COL TOM MCKINNEY

Yes ma'am. Can we go to sleep, now?

ANNA LEE

Tom, I mean really apologize. I want you to promise that you will apologize and I want you to compensate him far, far and away more than four thousand dollars. I want you to compensate him with some life changing amount of money. I don't think he and Sandy and their kids have ever had any money to speak of in their lives. Who better than his best friend to change all that?

COL TOM MCKINNEY

Okay.

ANNA LEE

Tom, I mean it from the depth of my soul. This time you apologize. You don't get in any fight. And no matter what he says, you just say you're sorry.

COL TOM MCKINNEY

I said I would. How many times do I have to say "okay."

ANNA LEE

And you're going to come up with some kind of compensation like I said, too.

COL TOM MCKINNEY

If I say, "yes" will you let me go to sleep?

ANNA LEE

Thank you, sweet………

ANNA LEE is interrupted by the clinking sound in the wall.

COL. MCKINNEY
What the hell is that noise, anyway?

ANNA LEE
I don't know, but it seems like I hear it even more often now.

COL. MCKINNEY gets out of bed, turns on a couple of lights. He walks over to the wall and bangs on a couple of spots. The third time that he pounds on the wall, he hears another clinking sound.

COL. MCKINNEY
Right here. Right between these studs.

COL. MCKINNEY walks out to the hallway where remodelers have left their tools. He picks up a circular saw with it's cord and brings it back into the room. He finds a wall socket and begins to plug it in.

ANNA LEE
What are you going to do? Tom, you're not going to cut a hole in the wall?!

COL. MCKINNEY
As a matter of fact, I am.

COL. MCKINNEY begins cutting into the wall. We see him cut an area from six feet up the wall, across an area between widely spaced old studs, then all the way to the floor. When he gets to the floor, he makes another cut all the way back to the first stud, creating what might look like a makeshift door in the wall. He then puts the saw down and takes the wall with both hands and begins to pull it back. At first we hear the wall cracking on the "hinge points" then he seems to quickly snap the wall open.

We see a vast area within the wall, but we are shocked as a mummified body falls forward and fills the screen. The body seems to be hung up on something that is holding it in a nearly upright position.

As soon as the body falls forward we hear:

ANNA LEE
Screams.

As ANNA LEE screams, we see her standing up in the bed and backing up against the headboard. At the same time, COL MCKINNEY has fallen backward onto the floor.

ANNA LEE

Tom, what is it?!

COL. MCKINNEY
Gees. What the hell? Baby, I don't know what it is.

COL. MCKINNEY starts standing up. As he gets up, HANNA enters the room.

HANNA

Mom, are you okay?

She sees the body.

HANNA

Screams.

HANNA runs to the bed and embraces ANNA LEE. As she jumps up on the bed, JONATHAN enters the bedroom.

JONATHAN
Is everything okay?

He sees his mother and sister on the bed. Then as he turns slightly, he too sees the body hanging out of the wall.

Cont. JONATHAN
Holy crap! What the hell is that?!

JONATHAN backs up slowly to the nearest wall. EVERYONE IN THE ROOM stands quietly and stares at the horrific sight of the mummified body. After awhile, JONATHAN walks up to the body and begins to study it more closely.

HANNA (scolding)
Don't touch it, Jon!

JONATHAN leans in closely and begins to rub the flat brass belt buckle on the corpse. When he does, we see the letters, "M M."

136

JONATHAN AND COL. MCKINNEY (simultaneously)
Malcolm McKinney.

After another moment of silence…

HANNA
What's a Malcolm McKinney?

Again, there is silence in the room. After an uncomfortable period of silence, we once again hear the clinking sound. This time, however, we see a few gold coins falling down out of the wall onto the floor. After a few coins have fallen EVERYONE IN THE ROOM continues to stand in silence staring. Then, a few more coins fall. After another long and silent pause we see a more steady flow of coins falling out of the wall.

This scene continues with ALL FAMILY MEMBERS standing still and silent watching events unfold.

The coins seemed to increase their spillage rate and again stop. After this happens a few times, there is suddenly a deluge of coins that spill out of the wall. Just as we believe that it is the end of the spill, we hear another racket in the wall. We then see a pistol (revolver) tumble from the top of the opening. When it hits the floor, it FIRES. We then see:

-a spindly table leg get blown off and
-the table begins to tip. As the table tips, we then see
-a pitcher of water slide off onto the floor, followed by
-a double-globed glass lamp and
-a few other knick-knacks. When
-the lamp crashes to the floor, we see
-sparks flying in the spilled water. The
-sparks immediately ignite the sheer drapes. As quickly as the   -drapes explode into flames,
-the fire burns out.

Still, EVERYONE IN THE ROOM is standing statuesque and silent. Again, there is an uncomfortably long period of silence, when, at last, the body of MALCOLM MCKINNEY crashes to the floor.

HANNA (quietly)
Why did daddy cut a hole in the wall?

After another moment of silence.

Cont. HANNA

Mom, is family night about over?

ANNA LEE

Tom, we're going down stairs.

ANNA LEE and HANNA begin leaving the room.

HANNA

Mom, who is Malcolm McKinney? Why is he in our wall?

COL. MCKINNEY

Jon, get some old sheets and call down to BENNNETT and
have him send some boys up here to carry this body out to
the barn.

JONATHAN begins to leave the bedroom.

Cont. COL MCKINNEY

Jon, bring a pillow case, too. Let's try to gather up all this
gold before we get a house full of people.

JONATHAN

Yes, Sir.

INT. – INSIDE THE HOUSE – LIVING ROOM – WELL LIGHTED.
NIGHT.

We see ANNA LEE and HANNA sitting on the sofa. ANNA LEE has her
arm around HANNA.

ANNA LEE

I think he was maybe your great, great, grandfather. He
apparently went missing on the very day of his father-in-
law's funeral. No one ever knew what happened to him.
Until tonight.

HANNA

Well, why was he in the wall?

ANNA LEE

I don't know. I guess that was where he hid the gold.
Somehow, he got killed trying to get to where it was hidden.
Maybe he fell.

138

In any case, it explains why all that part of the house was closed off until after World War one. In the late 1800's and I guess early 1900's they thought there was a dead cat somewhere up there.

                    HANNA
Oh, gross. I can't believe this. That's the most horrible thing I have ever seen.

                 Cont. ANNA LEE
Your grandmother, Rebecca remodeled all those rooms. Then, she gave that one to her baby boy: your father.

We see HANNA staring vacantly for just a moment.

                    HANNA
Mom.

                   ANNA LEE
What, baby?

                    HANNA
Just think. What about all those years daddy was in the war or off doing whatever he does, and…

                   ANNA LEE
Enough, HANNA.

                    HANNA
(Animated grimness) And you were in that bedroom all night…

                   ANNA LEE
Stop it, HANNA. Stop.

                    HANNA
And just inside the wall was a dead body, Mom!

                   ANNA LEE
I said, shush!

                    HANNA
That old dead corpse was just feet away from…

ANNA LEE puts her hands around HANNA'S neck and begins to gently squeeze.

                    ANNA LEE
One of these days, I am going to pinch your pretty little head right off your shoulders.

As ANNA LEE seems to stare, HANNA stares right back and mockingly puts her hands around ANNA LEE'S neck.

                    HANNA
And, one of these days, maybe when you're asleep, I am going to choke you to death, you evil old …witch.

For a moment we see mother and daughter staring at one another, then, HANNA leans in and gently kisses her mother on the lips. ANNA LEE again puts her arms around HANNA who rests her head on ANNA LEE'S shoulder.

                    HANNA
Will you sleep in my bed tonight, mommy?

                    ANNA LEE
Absolutely, without a doubt.

HANNA stares aimlessly across the room for just a moment.

                    HANNA (smiling)
Mom, do you think daddy is going to sleep up there in your bed tonight?

                    ANNA LEE
               (light laughter at the thought)
Probably. When they get that cleaned up and the body moved, he will probably turn out the lights and sleep like a baby.

BOTH WOMEN laugh.

                    HANNA
I love men.

                    ANNA LEE (indignant)

140

What?! What men do you know?

HANNA
Well, I mean. You know how everyone always talks about
how some men are so brave, bold and courageous? I think
they are just simple minded.

ANNA LEE
I thought you said you loved them?

HANNA
I do. I don't mean simple minded, like stupid. I just mean
they don't seem to have such complicated issues as women.
They get along with guys they don't even like. But women,
are always trying to figure out a way to stick a knife in their
best friend's back. For example, if I had a boy friend that I
mistreated, humiliated, embarrassed and generally treated like
crap and a lifelong girl friend... Well, if I fell off the side of
a ship, which one would throw me a lifesaver and which one
would throw me an anchor? You know what, I would bet the
guy would throw me a lifesaver.

ANNA LEE
Where do you get this stuff, HANNA?

HANNA
I think about stuff, Mom. I mean, my best girl friend since
fifth grade, just tried to steal my boyfriend. And, I guess she
did. I hate both of them. But, let's face facts, he did it just
because she, well. Well, mom, you know what a slut Jennie
is. She did it because she wanted to be mean to me. He did it
because. Well, I can't explain him, but I don't think he did it
to intentionally be mean to me. He's just a simple minded
man with a constant... Gees, mom. I'm afraid to say anything
to you. You and your bar of soap, thing, that you do.

ANNA LEE
(Sighs) HANNA, your father and I have been talking about
sending you to one of those really nice schools back east.

HANNA
Why?

ANNA LEE

Why, what?

HANNA

Why have you been talking about that?

ANNA LEE

Sweetheart, it's your language, the people you're around, the way you act like some loose woman. It's your unladylike behavior. You talk about things that are embarrassing and yet you seem almost shameless. We want you to be a lady. Someone who acts appropriate to your environment.

HANNA

Gawd, I hate family night. Why don't you send Jon off somewhere. Your little angel. He can do whatever he wants, say whatever he wants and you and daddy don't say anything to him. He gets a car and I don't. He gets to go to San Antonio by himself anytime he wants and I don't. It isn't fair.

ANNA LEE

Well, darlin'. You should know by now, he's our favorite, and you're not.

HANNA

I believe it. You and daddy treat him like he is some kind of god.

ANNA LEE

That's not true. Don't say that. Anyway we had a nice family night with everyone; didn't we? It's good to spend a little time with your family as you're growing up.

HANNA

Yeah, but our family nights always turn out like tonight.

ANNA LEE

No they don't. And, anyway, nobody got shot and we didn't burn the house down.

HANNA

So, is that the new standard of success for family night, that nobody gets shot and we don't burn the place down?

ANNA LEE

Well, you take it any way you can get it.

                    HANNA
I love you mommy. Do you think daddy will be okay
tonight?

                    ANNA LEE
I think so.

EXT. SAN ANTONIO INTL AIRPORT. A BRISK DECEMBER DAY.

SUPERIMPOSE: December 8, 1976

A beautiful P-51 Mustang is landing and taxis up on the ramp. Jon (Late
20's, almost 30) runs up to the airplane as COL TOM MCKINNEY crawls
off the wing. He is wearing a leather bomber jacket and is beaming with joy.

                    JON
So, how do you like it dad?!

                    COL TOM MCKINNEY
I love it! (Throws his arms around Jon)

As they are walking away a photographer is snapping photos.

                    JON
Happy birthday, dad. Mom hired the photographer. She is
going to have portraits made of you and her.

Directly in front of the airplane we realize a snapped photo is taken as it is
momentarily frozen (The photo will be copied into an oil painting). COL
TOM MCKINNEY is smiling with a great deal of happiness.

                    JON
Dad we've got to head for the Marriott, right now. We are
late and mother will have both our heads on a platter if we
don't get there soon. Plus the fact we're supposed to be in
tux-es.

EXT. MARRIOTT HOTEL. ON THE RIVER. SAN ANTONIO.
TWILIGHT

The two men are rushing into the lobby.

JON
Dad, I'll see ya later. I'm going upstairs to change.

INT. MARRIOTT HOTEL. JUST OUTSIDE ONE OF THE BALLROOMS.

A very large birthday party has already begun. There is music coming from inside the ballroom. Standing outside the room is ANNA LEE. She is surrounded by various friends who walk by and acknowledge her and then move inside. The lighting outside the room causes her to literally dazzle. She is dressed in an evening gown.

As she is standing there, we see the photographer, again. He snaps a photo of her (The photo will be copied into an oil painting). As the photo is snapped the camera broadens to allow us to see COL TOM MCKINNEY who has quietly entered the floor and is now moving up behind a large pillar. He moves slowly and places one hand on the pillar as he leans closer to it, seeming to hide behind it. COL TOM MCKINNEY is admiring the beauty of his wife, in all her glory. All goes SILENT for a moment as he looks at her. Then, HANNA (mid 20's) walks up beside him and links her arm in his.

HANNA
She's beautiful, isn't she. Daddy, you know, if it wasn't your birthday you would be in deep cow-patties right now. Boy, are you late for your own birthday party.

ANNA LEE sees the two and heads for them.

COL TOM MCKINNEY
Hi, baby. I was just going upstairs to put on that monkey suit you got for me.

ANNA LEE (Smiling)
Too late for that, cowboy. (Taking him by the arm) How did you like your little airplane?

COL TOM MCKINNEY
Oh God, Anna Lee. If you knew how long I have waited to fly that airplane... It's wonderful.

ANNA LEE
Well, it seems that the perfect gift for you is always a new airplane.

The two walk into the ballroom. COL TOM MCKINNEY is still in bomber jacket. The room applauds. The band begins playing. ANNA LEE AND COL TOM MCKINNEY dance slow and closely.

                    COL TOM MCKINNEY
          This may be the best day of my life, Anna Lee.

EXT. AIR FRANCE JET LANDING AT CHARLES DE GAULE AIRPORT. DAY.

SUPERIMPOSITION: PARIS 1984

INT. TERMINAL AT CHARLES DE GAULE. DAY.

MARIE and her husband, JOSH and TWO CHILDREN (9 and 10) are wandering into the terminal.

                    JOSH
          I am so sleepy. I think I could sleep for a month.

                    MARIE
          Not today. We are going to see Paris and all the shops and
          all the sights.

                    JOSH
          Can we check into the hotel, first?

                    MARIE
          If you must. I suppose the kids could use a nap.

INT. LUXURIOUS HOTEL SUITE. DAY.

                    MARIE
          Oh. Isn't this the most beautiful room you have ever seen?

                    JOSH
          At these prices it ought to be nice.

                    MARIE
          Look at the view. You can see all of Paris. Look, you can
          see the tower.

                    CHILD #1
          Mom, is there a pool?

MARIE

I think so baby. But I think it is an indoor pool. We can do that later, okay, sweetie?

CHILD #2

I'm hungry.

JOSH

Me too. Let's see if they will bring us a plate of snails. You want to?

CHILDREN #1AND2

Noo!

EXT. FRENCH COUNTRYSIDE. DAY.

The family is driving through the French countryside. The children are playing, fighting in the back seat.

JOSH

Are you sure you want to do this, Marie? Sometime when you dig up the past it can really bite you in the ass.

MARIE

I just want to see if I can recognize the place. Dad told me where it was. I think this is the village. Look. Let's stop at that tavern.

JOSH

Now, you're talkin', woman. A tavern is just what we need.

The car pulls up in front of a very old, rustic tavern.

INT. COLORFUL OLD TAVERN. DAY.

Inside we see the family enter the door. This seems to be a family friendly place. In the middle of the day there are a couple of older people sipping beer.

BAR TENDER
(he points as they come in) Americans? (laughs)

MARIE

Yes. Well, you may not be able to help us. We are looking for a farm, that I believe is farther up the road, overlooking the cliffs. My father was a pilot who was saved by two sisters who lived there during the war.

BAR TENDER
Of course. That's Antoine's place. The drunks, here, still tell stories of how brave the sisters were. When I was a kid I remember that everyone said the women had killed two Nazis. Now, if you ask any of these old timers, they will tell you that the women killed a hundred Nazis. Both of the women were finally killed, though. Later, our village bought the women headstones for their graves. They are heroes, here. The farm is about three miles farther up the road. Part of the old stone house still stands.

MARIE
So, we should ask for Antoine?

BAR TENDER
Oh, no. He died a few years ago. His daughter and her family still live there. She should be there, I suspect.

JOSH
Thank you very much for your help. We may stop back by for a beer.

BAR TENDER
Okay, but be warned, we don't have any American horse piss in a can! (laughs)

JOSH (Mutters)
Nothing like French hospitality. American beer has always been the best in the world. Buncha champagne sippin'...

MARIE
Before you get too carried away, remember that you're married to sweet little Marie Marquette, McKinney, Pinkerton. Born only minutes from where we are standing.

JOSH
Marie Marquette, McKinney, Pinkerton, is a boot-scootin', chicken fried steak eating, little Texas gal who can chug a long neck with the best of 'em.

EXT. FRENCH COUNTRYSIDE. DAY.

The family is again driving down the road. Marie is leaning forward looking
intently. We see the beautiful pastoral sight that seems so much more
pleasant than it did during the war.

>   MARIE
>   That's it. That's it. That is it; I recognize the place. I am
>   sure that is it. Pull up here.

>   CHILD #1
>   Mom, can we get out?

>   JOSH
>   Look around for dogs, first.

EXT. ROLLING FARM LAND OVERLOOKING BLUFFS OVER THE
SEA. DAY.

MARIE, sees the grave stones and begins walking toward them. A YOUNG
WOMAN-M is nearby working in a beautiful garden. JOSH walks up on
her. As he gets near, she turns and looks up. She is beautiful, she has a
beautiful smile and is about the same age as MARIE AND JOSH.

>   JOSH
>   Hello. Do you speak English?

>   YOUNG WOMAN-M
>   Yes.

>   JOSH
>   We're sorry to bother you. My wife wanted to stop and see
>   your farm.

YOUNG WOMAN-M smiles and turns to see MARIE.

>   JOSH
>   We are sorry to invade your home, but is it okay if the kids
>   pet the horses? They have horses at home.

>   YOUNG WOMAN-M
>   Of course.

148

YOUNG WOMAN-M stands up and begins to walk toward MARIE. She continues to speak to JOSH.

> YOUNG WOMAN-M
> May I prepare some tea for you and your wife?

> JOSH
> No, no, no. Thank you. I promise we will not stay but only a moment. My wife is familiar with your farm.

YOUNG WOMAN-M looks at JOSH with a mild puzzlement.

> YOUNG WOMAN-M
> Really?

As the two near MARIE, we see MARIE kneeling in front of the graves. There are three. MARIE is touching one of the stones gently.

> JOSH
> Honey, this is… I guess… (he looks at YOUNG WOMAN-M) well, I just assumed you are the owner?

YOUNG WOMAN-M smiles broadly at JOSH.

> YOUNG WOMAN-M
> Yes.

As YOUNG WOMAN-M's head turns slowly toward MARIE, we see her smile fade rapidly. She looks at MARIE intently. Her jaw drops slightly. We know that YOUNG WOMAN-M has seen something in MARIE'S face. Awkwardly, she reaches out her hand to MARIE.

As this scene occurs the camera is again close-up on MARIE. She has sensed that something is the matter, but is a bit perplexed.

> YOUNG WOMAN-M
> I am Marie Marquette.

As she says her name, MARIE suddenly realizes that something else has occurred. JOSH looks at YOUNG WOMAN-M in shocked amazement. He seems to shake his head. He looks at MARIE. He looks back at YOUNG WOMAN-M.

MARIE looks at her for an uncomfortably long time before answering.

                              MARIE
        My name is… Hanna.

                              JOSH
        Uh, I think I had better go watch the kids. (JOSH quickly
        leaves toward the CHILDREN)

YOUNG WOMAN-M stares curiously at MARIE. Then, after seeming
almost hypnotized she shakes it off. YOUNG WOMAN-M kneels down at
the graves.

MARIE kneels down beside her and continues to study her.

                         YOUNG WOMAN-M
        These are the graves of my mother, father and aunt.

We see flowers leaning up against the third head stone. YOUNG WOMAN-
M takes the flowers away and lays them on the ground. We see the stone has
the name Antoine Marquette and the dates 1918 – 1978. MARIE touches the
"1978" and looks at it with a bewildered look. YOUNG WOMAN-M looks
at MARIE almost passively and knowingly, now.

                    YOUNG WOMAN-M (standing up)
        I want to show you something. I will fix some tea.

                              MARIE
        No.(too emphatically)

                         YOUNG WOMAN-M
        Please. It is okay. Please come in.

The two women walk toward the farm house.

INT. LIVING ROOM OF FARM HOUSE. DAY.

YOUNG WOMAN-M brings a small box and a photo album into the room
and places it on a dining table. She takes out a photo of her father. She pulls
a few war medals from the box.

                         YOUNG WOMAN-M
        My mother and father were both considered war heroes in
        our village. My father fought the Nazis and was captured.
        He was held prisoner for nearly two years before the war

ended. My mother and aunt were credited for killing Nazi murderers right here on this farm. They also saved the life of an American pilot who landed here when his plane crashed.

YOUNG WOMAN-M, pauses and looks at MARIE.

                    Cont. YOUNG WOMAN-M
…but I guess you know about that part, don't you?

MARIE looks at the artifacts blankly and says nothing. Finally…

                         MARIE
So, your father came back from Germany and the prisons?
He lived til 1978?

                    YOUNG WOMAN-M
(weakly) Yes.

MARIE seems to gasp for air.

                    YOUNG WOMAN-M
After the war, my father came home to his farm. The town's people told him what had happened to my mother and aunt. They told him that the American pilot took his daughter to an orphanage near Bordeaux. These were letters that my mother wrote to my father before he was captured. His military unit sent them to us after the war. In one of them it tells my father that she is going to name her baby, Marie. I have read it a hundred times.

YOUNG WOMAN-M opens one of the old letters.

                    YOUNG WOMAN-M
You may not be able to read French, easily.

MARIE shakes her head gently indicating that she cannot read the letter.

                    Cont. YOUNG WOMAN-M
I would be happy to read them all to you.

MARIE looks blank and solemn.

                    YOUNG WOMAN-M

All of my life, my father told the story of how he went to the orphanage in Bordeaux looking for his daughter.

Again, MARIE seems to gasp for air, containing her emotion.

YOUNG WOMAN-M continues
When he found that almost none of the children had any possessions or identification he was heart broken. Then, my father would boisterously explain how he looked at the crowded room of children and saw me. He would brag about how the minute he saw my eyes he knew who I was. Over the years he would tell the story over and over. Everyone in the tavern down the road heard the story a thousand times. When I was older. When I became a teenager, I remember it angered me when he would tell that story. I heard it so many times I didn't want to hear it again. (Pause) Now that he is gone, I would give anything in the world to hear him tell it again.

(Pause) I guess that by the time I became a teenager, I knew I was not really his daughter. Maybe that is what angered me. I wanted to be his daughter, but I was sure I wasn't.

(Pause) My father drank too much. He was a wonderful father. He left this farm to me. I am getting married next month to a wonderful man. We intend to live here. He is a bank manager. (trailing off)

(Pause) You are Marie, aren't you? The American didn't leave you at the orphanage, did he?

(Pause) Today, when I saw you, I saw my father's eyes. They were the eyes my father was searching for when he saw me. I think I knew who you were immediately. I just couldn't figure it out at first.

MARIE
I'm sorry. I don't know what to say.

YOUNG WOMAN-M
I suppose this farm would have been yours.

MARIE
But, it is not. It is yours. Our father's daughter.

YOUNG WOMAN-M

It is a beautiful place. Someone said that it is equal to about
27 acres in the U.S. Does your family have a farm in the
U.S.?

MARIE

Yes.

YOUNG WOMAN-M

Is it as big as this? How many acres is your farm?

MARIE

Our family has a ranch with mostly cattle. (absent
mindedly)I don't know how big it is. It's very large, though.

YOUNG WOMAN-M

When my father picked me up at the orphanage, he took
hundreds of pictures. I would like to give you one of these.
You can see how happy he was. I never saw him happier in
all his years than in these pictures where he found his lost
daughter.

(Pause, then gently) Of all the orphans of World War two,
you and I were very fortunate, weren't we.

MARIE

Yes. Yes, most fortunate. (long pause) Thank you. I hope
you are okay. If I had known, I would not have come.

YOUNG WOMAN-M

I'm happy that you did. I had a wonderful life with my
father and I am most thankful for that. Come back whenever
you want.

MARIE

Marie, I will probably not pass this way again. You don't
need to ever concern yourself with me again. May God
bless you.

EXT.– TEXAS. LONG EMPTY TWO LANE ROAD – THROUGH
DESOLATE, FLAT TEXAS LANDSCAPE. BRIGHT DAY

At first, all that we see is the long, straight, two lane, highway in silence. Screen right: Texas road sign. After only a moment the silence is shattered by the sound and appearance of a car speeding along the road. The car screams past our camera.

INSIDE THE CAR

TIM CHAPMAN, in his late twenties is driving. He appears to be furious. In the passenger seat is ANDREA (ANDIE) LOTT. She is pleading with TIM. ANDIE is a very attractive, athletic young woman in her mid-twenties.

> ANDIE
> Tim, I don't care what you do. I just don't want to have anything else to do with you or your friends. You have to let me out at the next gas station. I am done with you and all your druggee friends. I promise I am not going to tell anybody. Just let me walk away from you. You're a lunatic. You're ruining your life and you're going to take down everyone around you.

> TIM
> Shut up. I don't want to hear anymore. Just…

> ANDIE
> You're just turning into a loser. A sorry, junky loser! You're ruining everything. I thought we were going to both be doctors, but you'll never make it as some hopped up loser.

> TIM
> Shut up! Shut up! Shut up! Why can't you just shut up?!

> ANDIE
> I want out. I want to never see you again.

> TIM
> You want out?! You want out?! I'll let you out! I'll let you out right now!

OUTSIDE THE CAR

We see the car suddenly veer off the road and travel recklessly across the flat prairie.

> ANDIE

What are you doing?! Oh God! Tim?! What are you going to do? Let's go to the next town and we can talk. Don't be crazy!

ANDIE suddenly reaches for the steering wheel and jerks it hard. For a moment the two fight over control of the car as it veers from left to right across the country side. After some fighting for control, TIM cold-cocks ANDIE. She is shocked and falls back against "her" car door.

CRANE SHOT

We see that the two have traveled far from the road and to a desolate sight. TIM slams on the brakes and the car slides to a stop.

ANDIE
What are you going to do?!

TIM
I'm gonna let you out! Come on!

TIM grabs ANDIE and drags her across the seat as he opens the door. ANDIE IS SCREAMING (ad lib). Without warning ANDIE goes on the OFFENSE and fights back VIGOROUSLY. The fight continues as the two fall out of the driver's side of the car. ANDIE kicks TIM. He doubles over. As his head comes down, ANDIE kicks him in the face; TIM falls backward. ANDIE jumps into the driver's seat and slams the door. In an instant, TIM is at the door. ANDIE locks the door and begins to start the car. With a large rock, TIM crashes the window and begins dragging ANDIE out by the hair. He finally gets a good grip on her and pulls her through the broken glass. Once again, ANDIE goes on the offense and the fight is seemingly an equal battle. At one point, it appears that ANDIE could actually beat TIM in this physical battle. She picks up a rock and while gripping it, hits him square in the face, once again dropping him to the ground. ANDIE is trying to open the car door (it is locked). TIM grabs her. She pulls loose and runs. Just as she gets to the edge of a "small" precipice (ravine, bluff – only a few feet deep), she stops. It is at this point that TIM knocks her down (tackle) and beats her brutally until she is still. TIM is so worn out that he can hardly muster the energy to move. ANDIE is lying on the edge of the "bluff." With one foot, TIM pushes her over the side. We see that she only rolls a few feet down the wall of the ravine.

(LOW CRANE/BOOM) SHOT FROM OVER TIM'S RIGHT SHOULDER

We are looking over TIM'S right should at ANDIE'S body lying partially down the side of the ravine. Slowly, the camera begins to move from the right to the left with TIM'S head as the center of focus. As the camera continues to move we begin seeing TIM'S VERY BLOODY FACE.

BOOM DISCOVERY SHOT

The camera continues it's rotation, but as it does we see (blur pan) (B.G.)THREE STILL DARK FIGURES ON DARK HORSES (FORBODING) over TIM'S right shoulder. The camera slowly continues it's rotation and then stops on a head-on close-up of TIM. In TIM'S eyes and other expressions he very slowly senses the presence of others. As he stands, breathing heavily, there is surprisingly, a rope (lasso) landing around him which falls open to his feet. TIM turns to see the THREE DARK FIGURES (BANDITS #1, #2 and #3). When he turns, he is frightened by the sight of three foreboding figures, he is immediately caught up by the lasso around his feet which BANDIT #3 pulls tight and jerks TIM to the ground.

                    TIM
          Wait! Wait! I have money! Wait! What do you want?! I can
          give you anything!

TIM is trying to sit up and is attempting to loosen the lasso. BANDIT #3 kicks him in the face. BANDIT #3 quickly wraps the other end of the rope to the rear bumper of TIM'S car. BANDIT #3 gets into the car and puts it in gear.

                    TIM
          NO, NO, NO, NO! Please! Stop! I have money! I have a lot
          of money!

As the car "tears out," we see TIM being jerked hard as the slack in the rope is exhausted.

                    TIM
          (Blood-curdling scream of pain)

BANDITS #1 and #2 (and the third bandit's horse) chase the speeding car. We hear BANDIT'S #1 and #2 laughing as they chase the car and TIM'S "body" which is being dragged aimlessly around the country.

EXT. RANCH NORTH BARN AND AREA BACK TOWARD THE HOUSE. DAY.

156

COL. MCKINNEY closes and locks a gate near the barn. He appears to be taking care of a few menial items. The general theme of this scene is calmness and a generally lazy, slow moving day. After dealing with the gate or other similar activity, COL. MCKINNEY begins walking back to the main house. COL. MCKINNEY'S jet comes overhead, low with the gear extended. He looks up at the plane.

INT. FROM THE KITCHEN OF THE MAIN HOUSE. DAY.

Inside the kitchen, we see ANNA LEE washing a dish at the sink and peeks through the window to see COL. MCKINNEY coming up toward the house. He draws nearer, then comes through the kitchen door (or door on the screened porch adjacent to the kitchen).

                    COL. MCKINNEY
        Well, I saw the jet coming in. The pilots will be up here to
        the house in a little while.

                    ANNA LEE
        Tom, I was looking for you. I yelled, but you didn't hear
        me.

                    COL. MCKINNEY
        What is it, babe?

                    ANNA LEE
        Marie called.

                    COL. MCKINNEY
        Are they still in Paris?

                    ANNA LEE
        They're coming home tomorrow.

                    COL. MCKINNEY
        So, how was their trip?

                    ANNA LEE
        They all loved it. I wish we had gone with them. It would
        have been so much fun.

                    COL. MCKINNEY

Anna Lee, like I already told you. I've been to France, and I sure as hell didn't leave nothin' there that I need to go back and see.

ANNA LEE

That was a long time ago, Tom. Oh, well. I'm glad they had a good time.

COL. MCKINNEY

Did, Marie say that they went out to her old farm house?

ANNA LEE

Yes, they did. Josh said they had a strange little surprise out there.

COL. MCKINNEY

What kind of surprise?

ANNA LEE

I don't know. Marie, said she would tell us about it when they get home. (Holding up a large lemon) Look at these lemons. Have you ever seen lemons like this? Do you want some lemonade, Tom?

COL. MCKINNEY

Yeah, darlin' that would be real good. (picking up a small stack of paper) I'm going to look at this financial statement out on the porch. Why don't you bring a couple of glasses out there and I'll tell you how rich you are.

ANNA LEE

Okay.

EXT. BRIGHT, BREEZY, LAZY AFTERNOON ON PORCH. DAY.

COL. MCKINNEY is reading the financial document. We begin to feel as though something should be happening. Only after a long period of silence, we see and hear the screen door being pushed open by ANNA LEE. She has a large tray with a pitcher of lemonade, a couple of glasses and other paraphernalia. She steps through the door and carries the tray to a wide-open area centrally on the porch. She has a very happy smile.

Suddenly, ANNA LEE'S expression changes dramatically. At first it looks like she has seen something awful. She stands statuesque for an instant.

ANNA LEE
(In a medium voice) Tom.

ANNA LEE drops the left side of the tray. Everything on the tray crashes to the porch.

Cont. ANNA LEE
Tom. (gasping) Oh Tommy.

ANNA LEE drops the other side of the tray to the porch. Her right hand clutches her chest.

(Medium shot and in slow motion) COL. MCKINNEY is seen turning to see ANNA LEE. He is shocked by her behavior. He begins coming up out of his chair.

(Medium shot, still in slow motion and in silence) The silence is broken now, with the sound of a TYMPANI DRUM with an extraordinarily slow two-beat cadence resembling a heart beat. ANNA LEE collapses.

The TYMPANI cadence is dramatically very-very slow and regular through the following very fast and otherwise silent scenes.

INT. PASSENGER CABIN OF JET. DAY.

ANNA LEE is lying on the sofa with an oxygen mask covering her face. One of the pilots is assisting COL. MCKINNEY as he kneels beside her.

EXT. JET IS TAKING THE RUNWAY AT THE RANCH. DAY.

For a moment we hear the sound of the jet engines in addition to the continued drum cadence. During the takeoff we realize the weight, energy and mass of all this power being focused on a life-saving mission. As the jet finally takes flight, the sound once again subsides and we hear only the cadence.

INT. HOSPITAL EMERGENCY ROOM. DAY.

At first we come through a very busy emergency room. However, we follow the gurney with ANNA LEE through another door where there is no one else. It is a very large/wide hallway. Nurses and doctors are chasing the gurney toward another set of doors which will open to the operating room. COL. MCKINNEY is touching ANNA LEE as she is being wheeled through the

159

hall. The entire party reaches the operating room doors. Someone begins to push COL. MCKINNEY back, indicating that he cannot enter. COL. MCKINNEY appears to be off balance. As we see his hand slip from ANNA LEE......

                    COL. MCKINNEY
        I love you Anna Lee.

The slow cadence continues. COL. MCKINNEY looks around as though he is lost. He is by himself. There are glass walls. Through one of the glass windows he sees what appears to be a doctor giving a couple of people some bad news. As he sees one of the people put their head on the other's shoulder, COL. MCKINNEY sees the sight as frightening and backs up blindly to the middle of the hall. The cadence continues.

COL. MCKINNEY looks around and sees the men's room. He loiters in front of it for only a moment and then walks in. He steps up to the large/long wall mirror, in front of one of the sinks. For awhile, he looks at himself blankly, without emotion. (cadence) After awhile he takes a deep breath and washes his hands and then his face. While he is dripping, he again looks up at the mirror. For a moment he looks helpless and beaten. He obsessively washes his hands and face again, very slowly, and thoughtfully. COL. MCKINNEY, looks around to dry his hands. He locates the automatic hand dryer (electric blower). He seems clumsy and slow to deal with the device. For a moment, COL. MCKINNEY stops and looks at the dryer, then, surprisingly and with seemingly little effort, rips it out of the wall and throws it to the other end of the restroom.

As the device crashes to the floor, COL. MCKINNEY again turns to the mirror and stands silent peering at himself. He is empty. There is no sign of what he is thinking. He is oddly just standing and looking at himself in the mirror.

During all of this the cadence has slowly continued, until finally, while he is staring in the mirror, we hear only one-half of the two-beat cadence. It has stopped. We are left in total silence for awhile.

Then, sound is added to the scene, again. Out of the silence is a song (same as or similar to)"Let it be me." The song is sung by a male voice.

        (V.O.-Song)- As clearly as a distant church bell, breaking
        the silence.
        I blessed the day I met you...
        Cont...

160

As the song begins, COL. MCKINNEY wanders out of the restroom. He reaches the middle of the hall and looks up. One of the doctors comes out of the operating room.

>   (V.O.-Song)
>   Now and forever...

The song pauses...

We see the doctor from the far end of the hall. When he sees COL. MCKINNEY, he inadvertently looks away and down. We know it is an ominous gesture.

CLOSE UP

We see an expressionless COL. MCKINNEY. Simultaneously the song continues.

>   (V.O.-Song)
>   Let it be me.

EXT. GRAVESIDE. DAY.

Continuing from the close up of COL. MCKINNEY, the camera backs away to a medium shot where we find that we are now at the graveside services. Hanna is leaning against her father.

The song continues as the camera slowly proceeds by the mourners. Significantly, we see the grief of a number of the ranch hands, particularly two or three who were with her and helped take care of her back in 1944 when she shot the foreman, SPIKE.

>   (V.O.) "Let it be me."
>   The song concludes.

INT. MAIN LIVING ROOM, DINING ROOM OF MAIN HOUSE – WAKE. DAY.

A large number of people are in the house at the conclusion of the funeral. The camera moves around the room and comes to COL. MCKINNEY AND MARIE. MARIE is leaning in close to talk to her father.

>   MARIE

Dad, are you sure you are going to be alright. I really don't like the idea of you riding off by yourself after all this. Why don't you come to San Antonio and stay with me and Josh and the kids for awhile. Hanna is going to stay with us. We could just make it a big family get together for awhile.

COL. MCKINNEY

Thanks, sweetheart, but I really do want to go out and ride for a few days. Do you think Hanna is going to be okay? I mean, if Hanna wanted to stay at the house, I would probably stay here with her.

MARIE

Do you want her to stay here?

COL. MCKINNEY
(looks at MARIE seriously)
I really want to saddle TRAVIS up and spend a few days by myself.

MARIE

Okay.

Later, we see JON walk up to his father.

JON

Dad, day after tomorrow, I am going to go ahead and fly over to Atlanta on that project we have working. Are you going to be okay here?

COL. MCKINNEY

I told Marie and Hanna that I'm going to ride TRAVIS out through the brush a few days and look around.

JON

Is that a good thing to do? I mean, isn't that dangerous? Are you going to ride by yourself?

COL. MCKINNEY

I know this place like the back of my hand. I grew up out there on a horse. It's just been a long time, now. I been meaning to. This seems like a better time than any other. You think little Hanna is going to be alright?

162

JON

Well, we're all upset. She's going to stay with Marie.
That's probably best.

COL. MCKINNEY

You know what Marie told me?

JON

About what?

COL. MCKINNEY

Their trip to France.

JON

What about it?

COL. MCKINNEY

She said she found out that her real father was a POW. He
came back home after the war and lived til 1978.

JON

So, (hesitantly and focused intently on his father) what do
you think about that, Dad?

COL. MCKINNEY

I don't know. I'll never be sorry that I brought that little girl
home with me. Do you think it was a bad thing that I stole
her out of France in a duffle bag? Apparently, her real dad
went lookin' for her and died believin' he had found her.

JON stood quietly looking at his father. Then, after awhile...

JON

Did she say why she decided to tell you that?

COL. MCKINNEY

I don't think she was going to tell me, but Josh said
something that caused her to. I guess now it doesn't matter
so much; does it?

She was telling me how much she loved Anna Lee and me
for being such good parents. She said she was sorry that she
used to argue so much with Anna Lee. I told her every
woman in this house has always fought with all the other

women. She rolled her eyes at me when I said it, but it's the truth. I used to worry that Anna Lee and Hanna would just up and kill each other.

                          JON
I know Marie has always been happy being the big sister. This is the only life she has ever known. She is as happy as me and Hanna ever could be. You're not upset about this too, are you?

                    COL. MCKINNEY
No. ...I may never be upset about anything again.

EXT. FRONT PORCH. RANCH. SAME DAY.

                     COOP SAMSON
Tom, I know we've had problems over the last few years, but man I cannot find the words to tell you how sorry I am for you and Anna Lee.

                   COL TOM MCKINNEY
Oh, thanks, Coop.

                     COOP SAMSON
She was just the finest woman any man could ever hope to marry.

                   COL TOM MCKINNEY
Yeah, she was. In fact, Coop, there was one thing that Anna Lee made me promise her. I promised her and then I ended up puttin' it off. But, I want to do it. And, well, I want to do it right here today.

                     COOP SAMSON
What's that?

                   COL TOM MCKINNEY
Well, Anna Lee wanted me to apologize for cuttin' your stupid finger off. But, the thing is, Coop. Well, I really do apologize. When you sued me, it kind of pissed me off I guess. But the truth is, I just want us to be friends again. Anyway, you and me both know it was your fault for stickin' your finger out there.

164

COOP SAMSON

My fault!? You asshole. You cut my damned finger off with
an ax. Whoever heard of dressing a deer out with an ax?

COL TOM MCKINNEY

You know; what you don't know would fill a library. I was
just tryin to break the sternum... oh, what the hell. You're
the one who stuck his finger in front of a drunk, swingin' an
ax.

COOP SAMSON

So, here we go. It's always somebody else's fault; isn't it,
Tom? By the way, if you were so sweet and innocent, how
come you threatened Judge Perry and got the case thrown
out, huh?

COL TOM MCKINNEY

Dammit. I never threatened nobody.

COOP SAMSON

Old Judge Perry thought you had a picture of him when he
was chasin' that girl through the whorehouse down in
Reynosa. I told him you didn't get any pictures, but he
wouldn't believe me. You must have convinced him!

COL TOM MCKINNEY

I did no such thing. And, furthermore, if I did have a picture
of Perry running naked through a whorehouse, I can tell you
that I sure wouldn't keep it as a souvenir.

COOP SAMSON

Actually, he was wearin' boots.

COL TOM MCKINNEY

Blue boots.

Both men laugh.

COOP SAMSON

Where the hell do you go to buy, blue boots?

COL TOM MCKINNEY

I sure as hell wouldn't want to be caught dead in a Mexican
whorehouse wearin' blue boots. (Laughs)

The two men stand quietly on the porch. Each gazes off into the distance. COL MCKINNEY lights a thin cigar.

Cont. COL TOM MCKINNEY
Well, Coop. (Pause) Anna Lee kinda always figured that the day I apologize to you, I would probably screw it up and get into another fight. She told me that no matter what happens, I should apologize and really mean it. You know how I am Coop. You've known me as long; well, actually even longer than Anna Lee. Bennett told me that everybody thinks I'm an asshole.

But, here is the deal, Coop. The deal is that we just brought in a gas well up north. It's gonna net out a lot of money for the next twenty years. I told my lawyers to transfer all the proceeds on that well to you and your heirs, Coop.

They said that you would need to sign some stuff showing that we are making a settlement for damages. They said if we didn't do that, you might get accused of something. You know, if it was just a gift.

COOP stands addled. His eyes well up.

COOP SAMSON
I don't know what to say, Tom. We've never had any money.

COL TOM MCKINNEY
Well, that's what you get for being the only honest lawyer in Texas.

COOP SAMSON
Tom, you're talking a lot of money here, aren't you?

COL TOM MCKINNEY
Well, depending on the price of gas; right now, I would say between one and two million a year.

COOP SAMSON
You can't be serious, Tom.

COL TOM MCKINNEY

I look at it like this, Coop. My family has more money than we can spend in a hundred years. You're as close to bein' a brother as I ever coulda had. If anything had happened to me before I took care of this, I would have been kickin' my own ass for eternity.

(After a pause) Did I ever tell you about the time I kissed Shanny Hollister.

COOP SAMSON

Only about a hundred thousand times. And, that was before 1941. Why would you think of her? You know she's older than you. She probably looks like an old prune, by now.

COL TOM MCKINNEY

No; Shanny Hollister is forever twenty-one. Guess I've just been feeling especially old, lately. I've been thinking of lots of old times.

COOP SAMSON

Tom. Sorry I sued ya. I shoulda just whipped your ass.

COL TOM MCKINNEY

So far, you're about the only friend who hasn't tried to kick my butt. Anyway, it's alright. I wish I had apologized while Anna Lee was here to know it.

COOP SAMSON

She knows, Tom.

EXT. - OUTSIDE THE BARN. MORNING.

COL. MCKINNEY is cinching up the saddle on his horse, TRAVIS. He also has a pack horse that is loaded with supplies. As he is finishing up, his ranch foreman Bennett, walks up.

BENNETT

COL., I wish you wouldn't go ridin' off by yourself.

COL. MCKINNEY doesn't answer. He appears mildly annoyed by the motherly attitude of BENNETT.

BENNETT

Well, I was just thinkin' that maybe I could send a couple of
riders with ya.

BENNETT waits for some acknowledgement, but gets none.

Cont. BENNETT

You know, Col. we don't allow any of the boys to ride
overnight alone out on the ranch, anymore. This place is too
easy to get lost, get hurt, fall off your horse or a hundred
other things.

COL. MCKINNEY

A man ought to be able to ride out on his own place.

COL. MCKINNEY gets on his horse.

Cont. COL. MCKINNEY

Bennett. (He pulls something up tighter on the saddle)
Bennett, if it makes you feel any better, I'll ride southwest to
the fence. From there, south to that old water tank. Then,
I'll look around a bit and head back along the south fence to
the creek. By the time I get around there, I suspect I'll be
out of coffee and whiskey, so I'll probably head back toward
the house. If I aint back in about a week, I guess you can
send somebody lookin'.

BENNETT

Yes Sir. (Pause) Col., you know, there aint a man on this
place who didn't think the world of Ms Anna Lee.

COL. MCKINNEY

You know, Bennett. Old Billy once told me that I would
have to find somebody as mean as him, someday to run this
place. All these years and I have never had to hire a foreman.
Anna Lee did something that nobody ever considered. She
just hired a really smart and honorable man to run the place.
I may never have to hire a foreman for the Tumbleton. Jon
will probably hire your successor, someday. That's fine with
me. You've done a good job, Bennett.

BENNETT

Thanks, Colonel.

COL. MCKINNEY rides off. He is leading a pack horse.

EXT.- VAST LANDSCAPE (AS MANY AS) FOUR VARIOUS CAMERA
SHOTS

We infer the view of a very lonely man who has decided to wander far away
on an enormous landscape. We see day turning to night. We view COL.
MCKINNEY alone at a campfire. Then, again riding through the day. After
a few moments, we realize that COL. MCKINNEY has been traveling in this
lonely land for several days.

Now, we begin to see close-ups of COL. MCKINNEY. He looks haggard.
He is tired and dirty. He has a sad and indifferent look on his face. We feel
even more emotionally tied to the pain he is going through, and yet, he has
not shown any overt emotion since ANNA LEE'S death.

EXT. "WINDMILL CAMPSITE" EVENING – DUSK - A SUNSET

There is a stark landmark windmill beside a water tank.

COL. MCKINNEY and his horse TRAVIS get within about twenty to thirty
feet of the tank when they stop and COL. MCKINNEY gets off TRAVIS. He
looks desperate. He looks to the darkening sky. We see and hear him huffing
and puffing like someone who is about to weep. Then, we are surprised as he
pulls out his revolver. His face is wracked with the pain from his soul. COL.
MCKINNEY – DOES NOT- point the pistol at himself, and he brings it
close to his face only once when he wipes his mouth with the back of his
hand.

Again, we infer bleakness.

As if mustering the strength, we are almost shocked when COL.
MCKINNEY suddenly breaks into weeping sobs. The impending build up
and then break to overt deep emotional behavior is out of character for this
man.

CRANE SHOT

As we see COL. MCKINNEY weep openly and completely we see that he
has traveled very far to the loneliest place on the planet to cry for the loss of
ANNA LEE.

He drops to his knees and continues weeping. After awhile, he begins to trail
off.

GROUND LEVEL SHOT –

COL. MCKINNEY is lying face down in the dirt. There is one camera angle that shows that he still has his pistol in his right hand and it is close to shoulder level.

CLOSE UP ANGLE

While lying prostrate, we see COL. MCKINNEY'S very dirty face LOOKING LEFT toward TRAVIS.

REVERSE ANGLE

TRAVIS is standing still and staring at COL. MCKINNEY.

> COL. MCKINNEY
> (to TRAVIS and quieter, now)
> What the hell are you lookin' at?

(Comically) TRAVIS snorts and then looks hard-away.

CLOSE UP on COL. MCKINNEY looking left.

FOLLOWED BY – CLOSE UP AS HE TURNS HIS HEAD (through the dirt) AND LOOKS RIGHT (still on the ground).

As soon as we see COL. MCKINNEY'S face when he turns to the right we know that he has seen something.

CLOSE UP – LARGE DIAMOND BACK RATTLESNAKE

COL. MCKINNEY is within feet and is face-to-face with a large rattle snake. The snake begins to coil and rattle. COL. MCKINNEY lies still staring at the snake. He looks at it curiously and without fear.

> COL. MCKINNEY
> (In a manner that sounds like he is quoting --)
> … the serpent asked, "what have you learned here on earth?"

COL. MCKINNEY stares for an uncomfortably long time at the coiling snake as it rattles.

We hear his gun fire. We see the snake fly. The gunfire is shocking and is <u>off</u> <u>camera</u> when fired. It is then immediately evident that <u>it is</u> COL. MCKINNEY'S gun to avoid any confusion where the gunfire came from.

Then after a short pause, COL. MCKINNEY continues.

>   Cont. COL. MCKINNEY
> Then, he said, "I have learned that opportunity cannot be
> long, and wisely pondered."
>
> (Exhaling into the dirt) Shanny Hollister. Nineteen hundred
> and (pause)thirty four. I kissed Shanny Hollister in 1934.

COL. MCKINNEY begins to pull himself up and go through the motions of setting up camp.

>   COL TOM MCKINNEY (V.O.)
> For some reason I started thinking about a lot of unwise
> decisions I had made in my life.
>
> Seems most of my best decisions were unwisely seized
> opportunities. Just flyin' by the seat of my pants. Lot of men
> want to live their lives over. I'm afraid if I did, I might end
> up doing it more wisely. That could be mighty boring.

SAME SCENE – DARKNESS HAS COMPLETELY SET IN. NIGHT.

COL. MCKINNEY has built a fire and stares blankly as he eats from a metal plate.

The camera angle begins putting the fire into the middle of the scene and suddenly starts backing away rapidly (zoom out). The fire becomes a very small dot in the darkness and we are viewing it from far away.

EXT.– VIEW OF THE CAMPFIRE FROM AFAR GLOWING IN THE NIGHT.

We realize now, that we are viewing the fire from very far away AND through the eyes of someone else. The person (through) which we are viewing the fire is breathing heavily. For awhile we stare at the fire and then we sense that we are moving toward it.

EXT. – WINDMILL CAMPSITE. NIGHT.

COL. MCKINNEY has wrapped up in bedding on the ground and appears to drift off to sleep. As he closes his eyes we also observe the burning embers of the fire grow weak and darken.

DREAM SEQUENCE - EXT. DAY – SURREAL IDYLLIC POND (PARTIALLY GREEN SCREEN GENERATED) SAME AS TOM MCKINNEY HIGH SCHOOL DAY DREAM.

Eighteen year old 18YO- TOM MCKINNEY leaps from the fishing dock. He goes completely under the water. Just as his head pops out of the water, he is face to face with MISS SHANNON (SHANNY) HOLLISTER. We see her bare shoulders above the water. Both are face to face with enthusiastic and admiring smiles.

                    18YO- TOM MCKINNEY
          (Softly) Hi, Shanny.

                         SHANNON
          Hi, Tommy.

                    18YO- TOM MCKINNEY
          I haven't seen you in almost fifty years. Where have you
          been.

                         SHANNON
          I have been right here. I have been waiting for you to come
          back.

18YO- TOM MCKINNEY and SHANNON begin to draw near for what is about to be a loving and sensual kiss when suddenly SHANNON begins speaking strangely to 18YO- TOM MCKINNEY.

                         SHANNON
          Hey, Mister. Mister! Hey!

EXT.– DARK WINDMILL CAMPSITE. NIGHT.

We see a close up of ANDREA (ANDIE) LOTT. She looks as though she has been beaten badly and generally is a mess. ANDIE is looking at COL. MCKINNEY who is beginning to awake from his dream.

                         ANDIE
          Are you awake? Hey, Mister, are you awake.

172

COL. MCKINNEY awakes looking at ANDIE. He is shocked by her sight and presence. In one extremely fast motion, he rolls out of his bedding and away from her. At the same time, he draws his revolver and in an instant, it is aimed at her.

> ANDIE
>
> Oh God! Please don't shoot me! Don't shoot! Please Mister! Don't shoot me. (Then much more calmly) I'm too damned tired to die, tonight. Maybe you could just shoot me in the morning. I might feel more up to it.

> COL. MCKINNEY
>
> Who the hell are you?

COL. MCKINNEY stares at and studies the young woman with a bewildered look on his face.

> COL. MCKINNEY
>
> Girl, you look like you've been hit by a train. Are you okay?

> ANDIE
>
> (Weakly, but defiantly) Do I look okay?

> COL. MCKINNEY
>
> You look like hammered round steak.

> ANDIE
>
> (She huffs or exhales tiredly) So, is that like some kind of kicker pick-up line, or something? Bet you don't say that to all the girls.

> COL. MCKINNEY
>
> Who the hell are you and what are you doing here?

> ANDIE
>
> Mister, I need some water. Real bad.

COL. MCKINNEY slowly holsters his pistol. He stands up, walks over and picks up a tin cup and throws a small amount of coffee on the ground. He walks over to a hand pump adjacent to the windmill and fills it with water.

As ANDIE is taking the cup she speaks again.

> ANDIE

You don't have a clean glass, do you? (She then gulps down
the water)

Can I have some more?

                    COL. MCKINNEY
Yeah. (As he fills the cup again) Did anyone ever tell you,
you got kind of a smart mouth on ya.

                    ANDIE
Yeah. I think that's what HE said, just before he beat the
crap out of me. You'd think I'd learn, wouldn't you? Have
you got anything to eat?

                    COL. MCKINNEY
(Staring at the young woman) Sure. There's about a half
plate of rice and bacon there. (He points) I was gonna have it
for breakfast, but I can do some more cookin' in the
morning.

                    ANDIE
Thanks.

ANDIE eats the food aggressively. COL. MCKINNEY fills the cup with
water again.

                    COL. MCKINNEY
Would you like some coffee?

                    ANDIE
You know what? I really think I would. I think that I am
suffering a little bit from caffeine withdrawal. My head just
won't stop pounding.

                    COL. MCKINNEY
Well, girl, if you're what caffeine withdrawal looks like,
remind me not to ever stop drinking coffee.

ANDIE looks up at him and stops chewing for just a moment.

                    Cont. COL. MCKINNEY
Hey. I'm sorry darlin'. I didn't mean to hurt your feelings.
Somebody really hurt you bad, it looks like. I think we need
to clean you up a bit and see how bad you really are hurt.

COL. MCKINNEY goes through all the actions of making coffee. Then gets a wet towel and begins cleaning her face and hair and arms.

Cont. COL. MCKINNEY
(As he looks her face over) Well, you are bruised up pretty bad, but even with all that I can see you really are a pretty little heifer. You got any broke bones?

ANDIE
I think so. I think I have one broken rib. But, the good news is that it is in place and is not moving.

COL. MCKINNEY
Really?

ANDIE
I'm a doctor. Actually, I'm doing my last year intern in Lubbock.

COL. MCKINNEY
Really. So, your boyfriend brought you out here, beat you half to death and left you?

ANDIE
That's about it. I've been wandering around out here in this God-forsaken place for days. I thought I was dead. Then, tonight I saw your fire and started walking. After the fire went out I thought I wasn't going to find you, but then I saw the silhouette of the windmill and figured you might be here. Mister, I really am glad I found you. I know I do sometime sound a little rough, but I don't mean anything by it.

COL. MCKINNEY
Well, one of my neighbors has a place about a day's ride southwest of here. It'll be the closest place to get a phone and we can get a ride back to where I live. We can have your boyfriend arrested before you go home. I think my daughter has some clothes left in her old room that might fit you. And, if you want, we'll get another doctor out to the place to take a look at you. Do you think you can sit on that horse over there for a day? Maybe a day and a half?

ANDIE

Sure.

ANDIE starts sipping the hot coffee.

> ### Cont. ANDIE
> Oh God, this is wonderful. I can't tell you how bad I needed some caffeine. My head already feels better. (Pause) My name is ANDIE.

> ### COL. MCKINNEY
> That's a boy's name. How come you got a boy's name?

> ### ANDIE
> Well, you're just a real charmer aren't ya?

She looks at him for a moment.

> ### Cont. ANDIE
> My real name is Andrea. When we were kids, my little brother couldn't work out the last two syllables so he called me ANDIE. I guess the name just stuck. But, you know what, I am twenty-four and you're the first.. well, the first person to ever say that I had a boy's name. Which, by the way, when someone calls you a heifer; is that a good thing or a bad thing?

> ### COL. MCKINNEY
> Sorry. Guess I'm just used to saying whatever the hell I'm thinkin' at the time.

> ### ANDIE
> It's okay.

> ### COL. MCKINNEY
> Well, my name is Tom McKinney. Everybody calls me Col. Tom McKinney. Kind of for the same reason you were saying. When I came back from the war, my old man called me Col. Tom at a welcome home party and the name just stuck.

> ### ANDIE
> So, are you a real colonel, or one of those Kentucky Fried Chicken colonels?

176

COL. MCKINNEY
Oh yeah. I was a real colonel. Flew B-24's in the War.

ANDIE
So how does an Air Force colonel, airplane pilot, come to be
a cowboy out here on the wild frontier?

COL. MCKINNEY
I've lived here all my life. (He looks at her curiously) what's
wrong?

ANDIE
Aw Gees!

COL. MCKINNEY
What is it?

ANDIE
I am about to blow bacon and rice!

ANDIE jumps up and runs away from the camp only a short distance. We
hear ANDIE –WRETCHING --THEN SPITTING. After awhile she walks
sheepishly back to the fire and sits down.

Cont. ANDIE
Well, COL. Tom. I'll have to say that your rice and bacon
was a whole lot better the first time.

COL. MCKINNEY
You feel okay, now?

ANDIE
Yeah. I haven't eaten in days and I guess the bacon was just
too rich for the system. I should have known, but I was
really hungry. Sorry. Hope I didn't offend the chef, too
much. The sad thing is that I am still hungry. I sure feel
better.

COL. MCKINNEY
I've got some bread. That will probably be good.

ANDIE begins nibbling the bread.

ANDIE

So, what are you doing way the hell out here in the middle of nowhere? I mean, we know why I'm here; I'm suppose to be dead. But, what about you? Why are you way out here by yourself?

COL. MCKINNEY

I haven't been out like this in years. Thought I ought to take a look around and see what's out here every once in awhile. The last couple of days I've found some broken fence. I wanted to make sure that these water tanks are all still workin' right. Stuff like that.

ANDIE

Sounds like kind of a lonely job. I can't figure why somebody like you would want a job like that.

COL. MCKINNEY

Oh, it's alright, I guess. Some guys really like this sort of thing.

ANDIE

But, you really don't, do you? I mean, I guess everybody wants to be alone sometime, but you don't long for that, too much, really, do you? You seem like somebody who is almost always around other people. Somehow, you don't fit the lonely cowboy scene, out on the lone prairie with the little dogies and eating off the chuck wagon and all that cowboy stuff.

COL. MCKINNEY

My wife just died.

ANDIE

Sorry, again. What about the rest of your family?

COL. MCKINNEY

All the kids left pretty quick after the funeral. I told 'em I was goin' to go out and ride for awhile, so they left and went home. They live in San Antonio.

ANDIE

What about your wife's family? Were they still close?

COL. MCKINNEY

They're all gone. I think her Mom died when ANNA LEE
was about twelve. She had a sister who ran their father's
trucking company, but then she died a few years ago. She
was young, too. I think Emily was only about fifty five when
she kicked off. You wanna try to get some sleep?

                    ANDIE
Okay.

                    COL. MCKINNEY
You look a lot better. I didn't mean to make you feel bad
awhile ago, but you did kind of surprise me. We have some
banditos that run along the border and then come up here on
this place sometime. They're dangerous, so I kind of stay on
edge about who comes around at night.

EXT. THE WINDMILL CAMPSITE. MORNING

COL. MCKINNEY has saddled TRAVIS and is putting a thick pad on the
back of the pack horse.

                    COL. MCKINNEY
ANDIE, do you think you can sit on this pack horse without
a saddle.

                    ANDIE
Are you kidding? I can ride bareback. That's the one thing I
do know about the wild frontier; is how to ride a horse.

                    COL. MCKINNEY
Ladies shouldn't ever ride a horse bareback.

                    ANDIE
Why not?

                    COL. MCKINNEY
Because.

                    ANDIE
Because why?

                    COL. MCKINNEY

I once knew a girl in a wild west show who rode a horse
bareback every once in awhile. It always made her ... well,
never mind that.

                    ANDIE
Well, now, you really are just a charmer with the ladies,
aren't ya?

                    COL. MCKINNEY
What do ya mean?

                    ANDIE
Nothing.

                    COL. MCKINNEY
You aren't goin' to go getting' all smart-ass again, are you?

                    ANDIE
No sir.

COL. MCKINNEY gives ANDIE a leg-up onto the pack horse.

                    ANDIE
What about all your supplies and stuff?

                    COL. MCKINNEY
Somebody will pick it up in a day or so. That is, if it isn't all
stolen.

                    ANDIE
Well, I'm sorry you're having to leave all your stuff out
here. Do you think you'll get into any trouble for losing it.

COL. MCKINNEY looks up at her for the first time realizing that she has not
concluded that he is the owner of the ranch.

                    COL. MCKINNEY
If you get tired of riding on this saddle blanket, we can swap
out and you can ride Travis for awhile.

                    ANDIE
I'll be okay.

EXT. PANORAMIC VIEW – RANCH LANDSCAPE. DAY.

180

COL. MCKINNEY and ANDIE are riding slowly across the desolate prairie.

ANDIE

You were right. A lady shouldn't ride bareback.

COL. MCKINNEY

Are you okay?

ANDIE

I'm okay, but my ass is worn out. I'll have to admit it's still better than walking. Yesterday at this time I was thinking about dying. For awhile I was thinking how I might kill myself, but out here, the only way to kill yourself is to keep on trying to live. You know what I mean?

COL. MCKINNEY

No.

ANDIE

Well, I mean you can't slit your wrists too easily. And you can't shoot yourself without a gun. Plus the fact, I forgot to bring a bottle of sleeping pills. When you think about it, it isn't that easy to do yourself in when you have been stranded in the desert. You just have to wait to die.

COL. MCKINNEY

Maybe that's the way God meant for it to be.

ANDIE

When I was out here the other day, I kind of thought for awhile that there wasn't any God. I felt like I was lost forever. You know what I was worried about most of all yesterday afternoon?

COL. MCKINNEY

What?

ANDIE

I thought about my mom and my brother. I was thinking that they will never, ever know what happened to me. And then I got really scared. I thought that they might think that I disappeared on purpose. Or, that maybe I ran away for some reason. I thought that they might think that I did something really awful and just ran away. It made me so sad, because I was pretty sure that I wasn't going to ever make it home. I imagined my mom crying on my brother's shoulder. That was when I kind of thought that there might not be any God.

DISCOVERY SHOT

From a front quarter shot of the two, we see in B.G., the black silhouette of THREE RIDERS.

                    COL. MCKINNEY
Well, you're gonna make it now. You think there is a God, today?

                    ANDIE
You don't seem that religious. Why do you think there is a God?

                    COL. MCKINNEY
For a lot of reasons. Everywhere I look, I can't really imagine that this is all just some big-assed coincidence. But, maybe the other reason is that this preacher I know told me something at Anna Lee's funeral.

                    ANDIE
What?

                    COL. MCKINNEY
He said that I will see Anna Lee again in heaven.

                    ANDIE
So, you believe that?

                    COL. MCKINNEY
You know what, ANDIE. I want to believe it so bad that I can't afford not to.

                    ANDIE
Well, I hope you're right, Col. (Studied pause) Look, over there.

ANDIE points to riders barely visible and seemingly riding parallel to their course.

Cont. ANDIE

Do you see them?

COL. MCKINNEY

No. See what?

ANDIE

Are you friggin' blind? Just out on the horizon. Can't you
see them. Are they the bandits you were talking about.

COL. MCKINNEY

Maybe.

ANDIE

So, we haven't made it yet, have we? Would they kill us?
Are they just thieves?

COL. MCKINNEY

I wanna ask ya something, ANDIE. If you thought they
were going to kill us could you put a bullet in their brains?

ANDIE looks at COL. MCKINNEY intently for a few seconds.

ANDIE

What are you asking me?

COL. MCKINNEY

Well, it's pretty straight forward. How serious are you about
living, today. I mean, yesterday you thought you were going
to die. What if you got faced with that same feeling again
today? How serious are you about living today? I guess
being a doctor and taking that oath to do no harm could
come into play.

ANDIE looks at COL MCKINNEY again for a long serious moment trying
to figure out the point of the conversation more precisely.

ANDIE

Look, Col. Tom, if it comes down to it and you have to kill a
bunch of guys, who are going to kill us… Well, take my
word for it that I am in your corner. If you're talkin' about
leavin' them out here for the buzzards, you don't ever need
to worry about me runnin' my mouth later about it. I mean it.

Oh, God. Are they going to kill us? I thought we had it made.

COL. MCKINNEY reaches pulls the revolver out of his holster. ANDIE sees it.

                    Cont. ANDIE
Oh Gawd, please don't give that to me.

                    COL. MCKINNEY
Are you crazy?! You're the last person I would hand a loaded gun to.

COL. MCKINNEY stuffs the gun under the saddle horn, between the saddle and the blanket. He then removes the holster from around his waist and puts it in the saddle bag.

                    ANDIE
Oh God.

                    COL. MCKINNEY
I see 'em now. They're a comin'.

We see the THREE RIDERS drawing nearer and nearer. Their darkness seems apocalyptic.

                    COL TOM MCKINNEY
They're going to cut us off right up there at that old shack.

EXT. FRONT OF OLD SHACK. DAY.

Just as COL TOM MCKINNEY and ANDIE arrive in front of the shack, the three bandits meet them by riding around from the other side to meet them head-on.

As this scene is laid out, we see COL TOM and ANDIE in front of the shack with ANDIE to the right of COL TOM and then the shack is to the right of ANDIE. Both are facing the three bandits.

BANDIT 1 gets off of his horse. BANDIT 2, nearest COL TOM, pulls his gun and points it at him. BANDIT 3, who would be nearest the shack sits grinning stupidly.

                    BANDIT 1

Good afternoon. Nice day for a ride, no?

COL TOM MCKINNEY
What do you want?

BANDIT 1
We decided that we need a new girl friend, senor.

You are not wearing a gun. You know, you really should.
There are all kinds of people out here, who are not very nice.
(laughs)

(To ANDIE)Get off your horse, Chiquita. (To COL TOM)
We are probably not the nicest people you will meet on your
nice ride, senor. But we do know what we want. And, that is
all we want. My friends and I have not seen a senorita in
awhile.

BANDIT 2 snickers. BANDIT 3 snickers. COL TOM MCKINNEY's eyes
lock in on the eyes of the man holding a gun on him. The two appear to be in
a staring game. We see BANDIT 1 drop his gun and holster to the ground.
He begins to unbutton his pants.

BANDIT 1
Get off the horse pretty lady.(He pulls ANDIE off into the
dirt.)

The two other bandits again snicker. COL TOM MCKINNEY and BANDIT
2 still have their eyes locked. As BANDIT 1 lifts her up and looks into her
eyes, she cries. Almost a minute goes by.

COL TOM MCKINNEY
Softly and quietly speaks to BANDIT 2
Is she naked, yet?

Just as the man's eyes involuntarily shift sideways, COL TOM MCKINNEY
pulls the gun from under the saddle horn in lightning fashion and puts a
bullet through the man's head. Almost simultaneously, we hear two more
rounds.

(INSERT FLASH FRAME)

COL TOM MCKINNEY looks perplexed. He cannot understand what has
happened. As he looks around, he sees that BANDIT 3 is dead and hanging

in his saddle. BANDIT 1 is lying dead and bleeding in the dirt. ANDIE appears to be in a state of shock. As COL MCKINNEY'S eyes rise, he sees a very fearsome wild man (JACK) standing on the porch of the shack. There is smoke coming from his rifle.

COL TOM MCKINNEY;
(Whisper) Crazy Jack.

JACK
Cousin Tom! Is that you, Tom?! (Laughing) You got old, Tom.

COL TOM MCKINNEY
Hello Jack. (He looks around) Thanks for the help.

JACK
Every time you come to see me you have some kind of problem, Tom.(Laughs) Is this a social call?

COL TOM MCKINNEY
We're just riding through, Jack.

JACK steps down off the porch and kicks BANDIT 1. As ANDIE is buttoning her shirt, JACK walks up close to her.

JACK
She's a pretty one, Tom! (He turns back to ANDIE)You stayin' for dinner tonight?! (He looks at COL TOM)We're havin' Mex'can food! (Crazy laugh) He looks back at ANDIE and laughs again.

COL TOM MCKINNEY
Jack. We have a long way to go. We're just going to ride away. Is that going to be alright with you? The girl is going to take that saddled horse and we're going to just ride away. Just like I did that night when my horse broke his leg. You remember that, don't you? (To ANDIE)Andie, can you get on that saddled horse? If you can't, I'll help you.

ANDIE crawls up on one of the saddled horses.

JACK
So, you ain't stayin' for dinner, Tom?!

186

COL TOM MCKINNEY
Maybe next time, Jack.

As the two ride away, we see JACK pulling BANDIT 3 off the saddle.

ANDIE
I'm afraid I might have peed in my pants, colonel.

EXT. RUNNING RIVER. DAY.

At a distance we can see that ANDIE is bathing in the river and then gets out.
She is standing by a tree where some of her clothes are hanging and she
begins to dress. As she is dressing, she realizes that COL TOM MCKINNEY
is sitting against a log idly and casually watching her.

ANDIE
You know, if you take a picture it'll last longer.

COL TOM MCKINNEY
Well, you know what they say. You never have a camera
when you need one.

She just shakes her head and then goes over and sits beside him.

COL TOM MCKINNEY
There is a bottle of Jack in the bag. (He points to a saddle
bag beside her)

ANDIE pulls the bottle (Jack Daniels) from the bag and opens it.

ANDIE
Speaking of -Jack. What the heck kind of freak show did we
just ride through?

She takes a big drink. Just as she swallows, she chokes on the vapors and
gasps for breath, simultaneously handing the bottle to COL TOM
MCKINNEY.

COL TOM MCKINNEY
You're supposed to sip it. It ain't frat' party Kool Aid.

ANDIE (catching her breath)
Oh, wow. I needed that, bad. (after awhile) Are we almost
there, yet?

COL TOM MCKINNEY
We're almost there.

EXT. – ARRIVING IN FRONT OF THE TUMBLETON RANCH HOUSE
– INSIDE LARGE AUTOMOBILE. DAY.

ANDIE is lying in the backseat of the car asleep. COL. MCKINNEY and
the NEIGHBOR are in the front. We see the car arrive at the front of the
house.

COL. MCKINNEY
Hey, ANDIE, we're here. Wake up. (He looks back up
front) Appreciate the ride. Come in for a drink.

NEIGHBOR
I gotta get home Col. Maybe next time.

COL. MCKINNEY
Sure appreciate the ride. Sorry for all the trouble. I owe you
one. One of the boys will bring a trailer for the horses.

NEIGHBOR
See ya later. (Louder) Glad to meet ya, Miss ANDIE.

ANDIE
Thank you so much. Please tell your wife thanks again, too.

As the car pulls away, ANDIE is looking at the house quizzically.

ANDIE
So, this place is called the Tumbleton Ranch?

COL. MCKINNEY
Yes. For about a hundred and fifty years.

ANDIE
So, do you live in this house?

COL. MCKINNEY
Yes, this is my house. Come on. We'll get you cleaned up.

ANDIE
Are you like the boss around here, or something?

COL. MCKINNEY

Well, yeah. I own this place. (He stares at her a moment)
You thought I was one of the hired hands, I guess.

ANDIE

No, I really never thought about it, Col. To tell you the
truth, I just thought you were the old guy in the middle of the
desert who saved my life. Somehow, I never really
considered who else you were. That's kind of odd, isn't it?
So, how big is this ranch?

COL. MCKINNEY
(Leading the way up the front steps)
About 440,000 acres.

ANDIE

Gees! Col. Even I know that's a lot. How the hell does
anyone come to have almost a half million acres in Texas,
anyway?

INT. FRONT, GRAND ROOM OF THE HOUSE

Cont. COL. MCKINNEY
Well, you start with a great great grandpa who wanted a big
ranch back when you could get one really cheap.

ANDIE
(Gently) Wow. This place is amazing.

As ANDIE'S eyes track around the room she is almost shocked at the
PORTRAIT of ANNA LEE. It is astonishingly large. She begins to move
toward it. Instead, of tilting her head up to see the painting, she seems to only
rotate her eyes upward as she views it almost reverently.

COL. MCKINNEY

My son, Jon, is having this painting moved to his office
building in San Antonio. They had another one done of me,
in front of my P-51 Mustang. The artist used photos.
Neither Anna Lee or I would pose for any such thing. This
particular picture of Anna Lee was at my sixtieth birthday
party at the Marriott in San Antonio. I married that girl
when she was seventeen. She was just as beautiful her
whole life long.

ANDIE

(Quietly) My God, Col. Tom, she was beautiful.

COL. MCKINNEY

(Pointing at some photos on a table)

This picture here is my baby, Hanna. She's finishing up
what's become a career, going to college, drifting between
Boston and San Antonio. This is my oldest daughter, Marie,
her husband and kids. And, this is my son Jonathan. He's
about thirty. He turned out to be a real business man. He
handles almost everything, now. Problem is, he kind of took
after his old man and chases around with too many little hot-
tailed girls. The kind of girls he couldn't ever bring home to
his mom. He'll settle down one of these days.

ANDIE

Well, he is a handsome critter. Guess he did take after the
old man.

ROSIE enters the room.

COL. MCKINNEY

Rosie, this is ANDIE. She will be staying with us for a few
days. Will you show her to Hanna's room? She will need to
find some of Hanna's things that fit. Please help her with
anything she needs. ANDIE, this is Rosie. She will help you
with whatever you need.

ANDIE

Hi, Rosie.

COL. MCKINNEY

Hanna has a phone up there. If you want to call your mom
again, or your school, or whatever. That phone hasn't had a
good workout since Hanna moved out.

ANDIE

Thank you. So, what? I'll see you at dinner?

COL. MCKINNEY

Sure, but you got the run of the place. Whenever you feel
like it you can explore this old house, or out to the stables, or
wherever you want. I advise you stay out of the bull pens.

ANDIE

Don't worry.

INT. HANNA'S BEDROOM. WINDOW. DAY.

This is the same room and same window used during scenes where MARY LOU also peered through the drapes. ANDIE leans against the window trim and peers out as the jet arrives low and slow (gear down) over the house on approach to land.

INT. BOTTOM OF STAIRCASE. DAY.

ANDIE has walked down the staircase where COL TOM MCKINNEY meets her.

COL TOM MCKINNEY

Jon has just landed down at the airstrip. He's going to spend the night here, and then be around all day tomorrow. Then, day after tomorrow, if you're up to it you can fly back to Lubbock. Jon needs to go to San Antonio, so they'll drop him off, then fly you on home.

ANDIE

Oh, wow. That's a lot of trouble for you all to go to. If I caught a ride to San Antonio, I could just get a Southwest flight to Lubbock.

COL TOM MCKINNEY

Don't worry about it. This is what you do, when you got your own plane. You fly friends home. (He walks away) He'll be up at the house in just a bit. We'll eat when he gets here.

(To Rosie, in the other room)
Rosie, we're 'bout ready for dinner. Jon's on his way to the house!

INT. DINING ROOM. EVENING, BEFORE DARK.

All three are sitting at the table.

JON

Well, Andie, I guess this is like early dining for you. Out here on the ranch we always eat the early bird special. I found that if I ever came in after six, all I was getting was left-overs.

                              ANDIE
We eat early at home, with my mom, too.

                              JON
It's cooling off outside if you want to walk around the place a bit.

                              ANDIE
Sure.

EXT. FRONT PORCH. DIMLY LIT. NIGHT.

ANDIE and JON are sitting in separate chairs on the porch.

                              JON
Tell me again, how you met dad.

                              ANDIE
Well, my boyfriend and I had a fight. He left me for dead and your father found me. I am feeling a lot better now.

                              JON
I was going to ask if you want to go riding tomorrow, but guess you have had all that you need of that sort of thing?

                              ANDIE
My side is better, but I'll pass on any more horseback riding, if you don't mind.

NEXT DAY. MONTAGE.

EXT. RIVERSIDE. DAY.

JON and ANDIE are swimming in the river close to the house.

INT. KITCHEN. DAY.

The two are raiding the refrigerator and making sandwiches.

EXT. WOODED AREA. OLD TREE HOUSE. DAY.

An old pickup is parked in front of a small old house where JON and
HANNA once played.

> JON
>
> I built this when Hanna and I were kids. We were together a
> lot. You would think we hated each other, but our older
> sister Marie kind of grew up and left us alone. We did lots of
> stuff. Some think we fight, but really we just give each other
> a hard time just for entertainment.

The two look at each other for awhile, but nothing happens.

> ANDIE
>
> Your dad said that you have had a lot of girl friends.

> JON
>
> Not really. He and mom just think I need to get the right
> girl.

> ANDIE
>
> So, you haven't been bringing the right girls home?

> JON
>
> I stopped bringing them home when mother and dad would
> give them the third degree. Dad wasn't so bad, but mother
> was hell on wheels when it came to who I should be with.

> ANDIE
>
> Sorry about your mom.

> JON
>
> She was the best. I'm afraid dad won't ever know how to
> survive this.

> ANDIE
>
> Really?

> JON
>
> He never shed a tear at the funeral. It's killing him, though.

ANDIE puts her hand on his shoulder.

EXT. FRONT OF AND AWAY FROM RANCH HOUSE. SUNSET.

ANDIE and JON are standing side by side on top of an old wooden flatbed
wagon (buckboard).

> ANDIE
> (Giving instructions jokingly) When you say how big your
> ranch is, you're supposed to reach your arm out, like this,
> and say, "as far as you can see."

> JON
> (Reaching out and then moving his arm) As far as you can
> see. (Pause) I've told dad that what I want to do is develop
> the ranch house area. Over there, we already have plans to
> build a Lion's Club children's' home. Then, the old house is
> going to be slowly converted into a hunting lodge. Down
> the river we are going to build some guest quarters for a kind
> of hotel effect. One day (he points) I want to build a golf
> course up that way and then bring the whole thing together
> as a resort.

> ANDIE
> Wow. You've really given this some thought haven't you?

JON looks at her and then holds out his arm again.

> JON
> And, the whole place will stretch from over there to way
> over there. (He passes his arm around and then puts it around
> her shoulder) (He looks at her) I learned that move in junior
> high school.

> ANDIE
> I think I remember that move. (She leans into him)

The camera backs away from behind, to a panoramic view of the couple
standing close together looking out at a magnificent Texas sunset. We infer
the beginning of passage to another generation as a phrase of the Title song is
cued.

INT. OLD BEAT UP PICKUP TRUCK. NEXT MORNING.

Inside the old pickup, COL TOM MCKINNEY is driving, ANDIE is sitting
in the middle and JON is sitting in the right seat. They are driving down a

very rough old dirt road to (what we view as a tremendously improved) Tumbleton airstrip (Long paved strip, large ramp).

                         JON
Dad, I have decided to go on to Lubbock with Andie, this morning instead of going to San Antonio. You remember we have that equipment over there that I can look at while I'm there.

                    COL TOM MCKINNEY
You don't have to make excuses to me for chasin' some pretty girl, boy.

                         JON
(Rolling his eyes) Well, I was just going to say that I thought I would keep the plane and crew in Lubbock for one night and one day. You don't have any problem with that do you?

                    COL TOM MCKINNEY
Nope. (Pause) Well, I'm going to go out and fly my Mustang this morning while its nice and cool.

                        ANDIE
I love this. I love riding in this old beat up pickup down a rough old dirty road. I love that we are going to your airstrip and I'm going to take a jet airplane home to Lubbock. It is – so- perfect. (She begins singing)

(Nervously and very animated) "I'm leaving, on a jet plane, don't know when I'll be back again………"

EXT. RAMP. TUMBLETON AIRSTRIP. DAY.

COL TOM MCKINNEY is leaning against the pickup. They are parked adjacent to the company jet. JON is loading his bag on board. ANDIE is standing in front of COL TOM MCKINNEY saying goodbye.

                        ANDIE
So, is that boy of yours going to break my heart?

                    COL TOM MCKINNEY
(Thoughtfully) He might. I'm not sure how much experience he has with a girl whose I.Q. is greater than her bra size.

ANDIE

Well, that still wouldn't give me any great I.Q. (Long pause
and looks around) I guess I should say thanks. You know,
for saving my life. (Tears well up)Thank you for everything.
No matter what happens, I will never forget you, forever.

COL TOM MCKINNEY

Well, a man couldn't ever ask for much more than that.

ANDIE

Guess it's time to go.

After a moment of hesitancy, she walks up and puts her arms around his
shoulders. She whispers in his ear.

ANDIE

I never met a real dragon slayer, before. (She kisses his
cheek)

(O.S.)JON

You ready, Andie?

ANDIE (Cont.)

Maybe I'll see you again, sometime.

COL TOM MCKINNEY

I'll have Rosie set an extra place for Thanksgiving dinner. I
figure Anna Lee would be proud to see her boy bring home a
girl like you.

ANDIE smiles and chokes back further emotion. She waves as she gets to the
steps of the airplane.

EXT. AIRSTRIP. DAY.

The jet roars down the runway and lifts off with the song, "Leaving on a Jet
Plane."

COL TOM MCKINNEY (V.O)

As it turned out, the loss of Anna Lee was a lot worse than I
expected. There for just a little while I thought I was past it.
But, I wasn't. One of the things I remember thinking was
that when I was a young man, I would never have thought of
asking for or expecting to find a wife like Anna Lee. It's

hard to describe, but she turned out to be a treasured gift so much more than what a young man would ever expect from a woman who would be a wife for forty years.

I recall that the first time I finally started pulling out of my deep dark, "lows" was when I started hearing myself say things out loud. I cursed the night because it was dark. Then, I cursed the summer because it was hot and the winter because it was cold. The anger that I directed toward the whole world finally just wore me out. One morning I woke up and didn't curse the sun for rising in the east. I remember specifically thinking how happy I was that I had been given such a gift as Anna Lee. We will meet again.

CRANE SHOT

The song fades and we hear the lonely-mournful sound of light wind. COL TOM MCKINNEY walks around the P-51 Mustang. A mechanic accompanies him around the airplane and watches him get in. We see the airplane start and then taxi to the end of the runway..

GROUND LEVEL SHOT

The Mustang begins it's takeoff roll. Just as it lifts off and comes over the camera, we hear the 12 cylinder Rolls Royce. Then, the song, "Wayward Wind" is cued.

AERIAL SHOTS (accelerated montage)

The dramatic aerial scenes are accompanied by the song. At the very end of the song, the airplane disappears for just a moment on the finale where there are a number of very hard percussion beats. The camera comes to rest at ground level, framing the horizon.

COL TOM MCKINNEY (V.O)
(There is a woofer vibration that we sense above and behind us. It is light at first and continues to crescendo "closer" throughout this V.O.)

A famous baseball player was asked to reflect on his life and career. He said, "If I had wished for it, I couldn't have wished this good."

I figure me and Johnny Bench are the only ones who really
know what that means.

SUDDENLY. We hear the aircraft from behind and overhead as it comes
back in at a low-level over the top and (re-enters the scene – we see the tail
of the plane) it is flying toward the distant horizon. The sound of the engine
is (high decibel Dolby - surround) dramatic. As it flies away in the distance,
the airplane is ROLLED once and then climbed up and out of the top of the
frame.

EXT. FRONT OF MCKINNEY OFFICE BUILDING. DAY.

Sign: "The McKinney-Tumbleton Corporation."

SUPERIMPOSITION

TEN YEARS LATER

INT. JON MCKINNEY'S OFFICE. DAY.

JON is on the phone. He is standing and simultaneously putting on his suit
coat.

                              JON
          Andie, I am on my way. Just tell Anna her daddy will be
          there in a minute or two. Okay!

IN MOTION

We follow JON out of his office, down a flight of stairs and by a large wall
where we see two magnificent oil paintings of ANNA LEE and COL TOM
MCKINNEY.

INT. SCHOOL. BACKSTAGE. DAY.

A number of children preparing for a school play. A nine year old girl,
ANNA is talking to her mother, ANDIE. ANDIE AND JON'S three year old
son is hanging on to ANDIE.

                              ANDIE
          Your daddy is on his way, Anna. You are going to do so
          good.

JON enters the backstage area.

ANNA (to JON)
Daddy! I didn't think you were going to make it.

JON
Do you think I would miss your Texas pageant, honey?

ANNA
I am so nervous, Daddy.

ANDIE
You sing so pretty, sweetheart. (Quietly) You're the best one here.

JON
It's true, baby. Do what I do, when I make a speech. Just remember the very first five words, then all the rest come pouring out.

ANNA
Really?

INT. AUDITORIUM.

ANDIE, JON are sitting in the auditorium with their son in a seat between them.

JON
Honey, does she really know how to sing this song?

ANDIE
Oh yeah. She can belt it out like a Las Vegas lounge singer.

The curtain opens. ANNA begins the movie Title song. As the small voice begins singing it is slowly and dramatically accompanied by a hundred voice choir and then a symphony orchestra. At the same time the following scenes (montage) are viewed.

EXT. ELABORATE AND NEW FRONT GATE TO THE RANCH. DAY.

EXT. OLD HOUSE WITH GRAND FACE LIFT. DAY.

EXT. CHILDRENS HOME. DAY.

EXT. SWIMMING POOL. WATERFALL. DAY

EXT. LUSH, GREEN, GOLF COURSE. DAY.

EXT. CABANAS ALONG THE RIVER FRONT. DAY.

EXT. VERY LONG SHOT. AERIAL VIEW AS THE CAMERA TAKES
ONE LAST SHOT OF RANCH LAND VASTNESS. DAY.

INT. AUDITORIUM STAGE. DAY.

As the end of the song arrives, the choir is taken away, and then the orchestra
is silent and we hear(ANNA), one small voice, conclude the song.

FADE OUT

Epilogue

Colonel McKinney would occasionally tell a family story of George Tumbleton finding the gold. For some reason this story was never mentioned in any of his last recordings. Most of the family said that they believed it to be a minor event in the family's history except for one important element that was recently found. The family story always included a man named Bowers with whom Tumbleton split the gold. The story also included the fact that Bowers wanted to return to Kentucky and marry his sweetheart, Bonnie May, or Bonnie Sue, or Bonnie Lee, or some other similar name.

Shortly after Edward L. Hawke wrote the screenplay, a family member was sorting through some of Anna Lee's sister Emily's possessions when they found a very old Bible. It had a record showing that on Christmas Day, 1836, Jethro Bowers married Bonnie Jean Clemmons.

The family is certain that George Tumbleton split his gold with Anna Lee's great (+) grandfather, Jethro Bowers. They are equally convinced that some form of divine intervention finally brought Anna Lee and Tom McKinney together in the twentieth century.

When Edward Hawke was asked if he wanted to revise his screenplay to discuss the matter, he said, "No. I think I'll leave that bit of trivia for Robert Osborne to mention late some night."

Finally, there was a discrepancy found during a corporate audit regarding the deeded acreage of the ranch. It was disclosed that sometime decades ago, approximately 10,000 acres were deeded to Maria Consuela Martinez and her son. Before his death, Col. McKinney confirmed that the 10,000 acres belong to the heirs of one of Malcolm McKinney's sons.

www.ingramcontent.com/pod-product-compliance
Lightning Source LLC
Chambersburg PA
CBHW031110260626

47172CB00001B/304